Don't miss the rest of the
BEN BRAVER series!

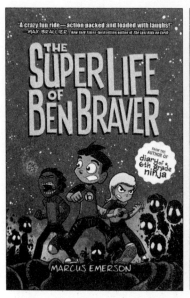

"Just the right mix of mystery and kooky fun."

—*Kirkus Reviews*

"Sure to be a hit with the comic-cartoon crowd and fans of superhero tales."

—*School Library Journal*

BEN BRAVER AND THE
VORTEX OF DOOM

Also by Marcus Emerson

The Super Life of Ben Braver

Ben Braver and the Incredible Exploding Kid

Recess Warriors: Hero Is a Four-Letter Word

Recess Warriors 2: Bad Guy Is a Two-Word Word

Diary of a 6th Grade Ninja series

Secret Agent 6th Grader series

BEN BRAVER AND THE VORTEX OF DOOM

By

Marcus Emerson

ROARING BROOK PRESS

New York

Published by Roaring Brook Press
Roaring Brook Press is a division of
Holtzbrinck Publishing Holdings Limited Partnership
120 Broadway, New York, NY 10271

mackids.com

Library of Congress Cataloging-in-Publication Data is available.

ISBN: 978-1-62672-712-0

Our books may be purchased in bulk for promotional, educational, or business use. Please contact your
local bookseller or the Macmillan Corporate and Premium Sales Department at (800) 221-7945 ext.
5442 or by email at MacmillanSpecialMarkets@macmillan.com.

First edition, 2020
Printed in the United States of America by LSC Communications, Harrisonburg, Virginia

1   3   5   7   9   10   8   6   4   2

FOR JIM AND SANDI . . .

Y ou see that?

That . . . is a black hole.

Or something like it.

It was more like a giant vortex of doom that was growing larger smack dab in the middle of Times Square in New York City. Not the best place for something like that to randomly appear, but that was the point.

It was one of those "end of the world" moments that always happen in movies. No superhero battle is complete without a massive hole of death in the sky, threatening all life as we know it, right?

Yup. That thing was gonna tear the planet apart. I'd love to tell you I had nothing to do with it, but I think you know me better than that by now.

I might be a *little bit* responsible for it.

But only a little.

I wanted to save the day, but instead, I set off a chain reaction that was about to lead to the extinction of the human race.

Whoopsies . . .

CHAPTER ONE

My name is Ben Braver, and I am a *nobody*.

For you noobs out there, here's the deets . . .

Two years ago, I was invited to Kepler Academy for sixth grade.

It's a super-secret school for super-secret kids with super-secret superpowers. The whole thing was super-secret. Obviously, I accepted the invite—because who could say no to that?

I was pumped!

Was I invited because I had a power?

Was I gonna *get* a power?

Was I gonna be *the Chosen One*?

The answers to those questions are nope, even more nope, and nope with some extra salt.

Turns out, the only people in the world who have powers are those born with them. And they're all descendants of the Seven Keys—seven peeps who were experimented on in a laboratory. None of them got powers, but their kids (a.k.a. "the descendants") did. And since I'm not a descendant, I'll never have any powers.

Bummer, right?

So why the heck was I invited to the academy at all?

Because I was destined to save the school.

Twice.

Turns out the headmaster, Donald Kepler, is a time traveler, and he saw a future where his academy needed a no-powered nobody like me.

He had seen a future where the world ended, destroyed by some jerk named the Reaper. But it didn't end, because Kepler changed history—and trapped the Reaper outside the universe so he could never ever become the bad guy. Kepler spent the rest of his life protecting this timeline from that terrible fate.

But now, I'm at Kepler's funeral.

And the Reaper?

He's back.

CHAPTER TWO

Ten hours ago . . .

So there I was, sitting in the last row at Headmaster Kepler's funeral on the very last day of seventh grade, roasting marshmallows on Noah's head. His hair had gone full Human Torch a few months back, and nothing he did could snuff it out.

Penny and Jordan were chillin' on the other side of me. You see Penny's arm around my back?

Yeah, no, I just wanted you to see.

It's not around *Jordan's* back.

Just sayin'.

Anyway, those three are my BFFs, but sadly, I knew it was the last day I'd ever get to hang out with them.

The school year was over, and in just a few hours, I'd be on my way back to my parents at home, never to return to Kepler Academy.

Don't get me wrong, I *wanted* to go home. As far as the school? I was over it. Too much danger for *this* kid.

I mean, I had almost *died* there.

Like, a *hundred* times.

But I wasn't ready to leave my friends.

Not yet.

We were all decked out because that's usually how it goes for funerals. At least I think it is. I'd never actually been to one.

Technically, I still haven't, because Kepler wasn't exactly dead. He was badly injured after saving me from a horrible explosion. If he'd stayed in our world, he would've died, so he escaped outside the universe. Now he's stuck there, alone in a place where time doesn't exist.

I'm still alive because of him.

And I never got the chance to say thanks.

Onstage, one of the teachers took the mic and started

in with a boring story about the old headmaster, but she was interrupted by a loud crash.

I got this gross feeling, deep in my gut—the kind that tells you to run away because something terrible is about to happen.

I'm really good at ignoring that feeling.

Students stood on their chairs, making it impossible to see what was happening from the back row, but I could hear it over the speakers.

I jumped up from my seat and tore down the aisle.

"Ben, wait!" Noah said. "What're you doing?"

"Getting a better look!" I said.

I stopped in front of the stage. On the center of it was a kid wearing an Elvis Presley mask, writhing around like he was wrestling something invisible.

And even though I couldn't see it, I knew what it was because the same thing tried to suction-cup itself to my head a couple months ago.

It was an invisible creature that ended the world in an alternate timeline, a.k.a. . . . the Reaper.

And then the kid stopped.

He ripped off the Elvis mask, frantically searching his body for whatever had been clinging to him, but when he shrugged it off, I knew it was too late—the Reaper wasn't on him anymore.

And it was obvious that the kid had no idea what he had just wrestled with—if he did, he'd be freaking out just as much as I was, but he was totally calm.

When he saw Headmaster Donald Kepler's portrait, he blew a raspberry and pouted. "I'm at my *funeral*?" And then he raised a fist.

The new headmaster, Raymond Archer, approached slowly. "Young man, are you . . . lost?"

"Nope," the boy said, vigorously rubbing his head once more to check for the invisible creature.

Still nothing.

The boy jumped from the stage and strolled back to the school like he owned the place.

Students mumbled, trying to figure out what was happening, but I already knew—it was Donnie Kepler, the eleven-year-old version of Headmaster Kepler. Donnie had been skipping through time, playing hide-and-seek with the older version of himself, and now he was here.

And he had accidentally brought the Reaper with him.

"Holy donks," I whispered.

I pulled my shirt over my head to protect myself and

frantically started searching for the invisible creature that was most *definitely* nearby.

My friends caught up with me as Headmaster Archer ran to the school, disappearing through the front doors.

"Bro, you gotta stop running off like that," Noah said. "Next time, wait so we can come up with a *plan*."

UMM, WHAT'S WITH THE TURTLE IMPRESSION?

My friends didn't realize the Reaper was with Donnie. They'd FREAK OUT just as much as I was if they knew. But it didn't matter because Penny was *clearly* freaking out, too.

She yanked my shirt down and stared at me with the fire of a thousand suns burning in her eyes. "What's wrong?? You're acting like something *horrible* is happening!"

I wanted to tell her everything. To tell her that the monster who destroyed the world was literally standing around us somewhere, probably thinkin' about destroying the world again.

But I couldn't.

Because, at that moment, the Reaper didn't know I knew he was there, which meant I had the upper hand.

I needed to get to Donnie. He was wrestling that thing when he bounced on the stage.

"I need to get to Donnie," I said. "Where'd he go?"

Noah pointed to the front of the school. "He's up there."

Donnie was at the buffet tables that had been set up for the funeral lunch. He was putting food on his plate like he *didn't even care* he'd brought the apocalypse with him.

Did he even know??

I was about to run to Donnie but stopped because Penny looked like she was about to have a meltdown. She was whipping her hands like she was trying to shake water off them.

"Are *you* okay?" I asked.

"*Don't worry about it!*" she said, mocking me, and then she shoved her hands into her pockets. "I'll catch up! Just go without me!"

She didn't have to tell me twice, so I started running.

"Ben, come on, man!" Noah said, annoyed. "*Do you hate plans or something?*"

None of the kids working the buffet tables seemed to care that Donnie was grabbing some grub, except for Dexter and Victoria—the academy's unofficial bullies. They were helping with the lunch setup, but only because it gave them first dibs on all the food. They glared at Donnie as he carefully stacked potato chips on his plate.

I stopped a few feet from him, not sure what to say.

"You guys still eat hot dogs in the future," Donnie said, grabbing one with his free hand. "That's so *lame.*"

"Why?" Vic asked.

"I just expected *more*," Donnie sighed. "Where are the flying cars? The floating cities? I mean, do you guys even live on the moon yet?"

Vic stared at the boy. "Who *are* you?"

"Donnie Kepler."

"No," Dexter said. "Donald Kepler's *dead.*"

"Right. *That* Donald Kepler's dead," Donnie said, nodding toward the funeral. "But *I'm* not."

Dexter and Vic looked like confused mules.

Donnie took a bite of hot dog. "Ew," he said. "Hot dogs still *taste* gross, too."

Apparently, that was the last straw for Dexter.

Dexter marched around the table, glaring at Donnie. "Now put that food back and respect the dead!"

Dexter grabbed Donnie's elbow—my cue to jump in. Donnie's face was about to meet Dexter's fist.

I grabbed Donnie's other elbow, but just as I did, a quarter-sized disc landed on his neck with a *THP!* It was one of the discs that Professor Duncan, our very own mad-scientist ghost professor, had created before he became a ghost.

He had a dozen different kinds of discs, each one color coded so you'd know exactly what it did. Blue discs teleported you. Red discs made you grow bigger. And pink discs straight up exploded like grenades.

The one on Donnie's neck was yellow.

I didn't know what the yellow ones did.

A surge of electricity suddenly ripped through my body. Donnie and Dexter felt the same thing as the three of us seized up in blinding pain.

And then it all stopped, and everything went black. So *that's* what the yellow discs did.

CHAPTER THREE

"**B**en?" a man said. "Are you all right? You look like you're about to blow chunks."

I shook my head. I don't know why, but I was tired. Like, *stupid* tired. The soothing sound of rain on umbrellas wasn't helping, either.

"Yeah, I'm fine," I said. "Sorry."

Everything was a blur of gray colors. I couldn't focus on the faces in the crowd, but I knew they were waiting for me to say something.

Where the heck was I?

"It's okay," the man said, putting his hand on my shoulder. "Take all the time you need. We're all here for you, buddy."

"Thanks," I said, turning to him.

Then I saw it wasn't a *him* but an *it*, and by *it*, I mean he was a gigantic lollipop.

In fact, *everybody* there was a different kind of candy, dressed up and keeping themselves dry with huge black umbrellas.

It suddenly dawned on me—I was at a funeral.

My *wife's* funeral to be exact.

My *peanut butter cup wife's* funeral to be even *more* exact. My friends and family were waiting for my eulogy.

I cleared my throat and did my best to keep from choking up. "Hey, everybody . . . thanks for coming. I know Buttercup's heart is filled with love and joy as she's watching us from peanut butter heaven."

The candy nodded, tears in their eyes.

"Yes, she murdered a peanut butter and jelly sandwich on our wedding day. Yes, she tried to kill me with a laser sword on our honeymoon. And yes, she was an intergalactic assassin, but she was still the love of my life.

All things, good or bad, come to an end. . . ." I cleared my throat. "And she will be missed."

The service ended.

Candy in the crowd took turns dropping flowers into Buttercup's grave before leaving.

But I stayed behind awhile.

I knew that when I left, it would *really* be over.

My life would never be the same, and I guess I just wanted to hang on to it, even if only for a few more seconds . . .

CHAPTER FOUR

"**W**ake up, ya nub," a gruff voice said.

I opened my eyes.

A bright light was shining right over my face. My body was killing me. Every bone ached, every muscle stung, and my hair smelled like I just came from a bonfire.

It was quiet, except for a television playing in another room. "*. . . and in other news—a bank robbery was foiled in Portland, Oregon, earlier today when witnesses say a boy jumped in front of a moving car to stop the would-be thieves. . . .*"

When my eyes adjusted, I looked around. I was in the nurse's office, and a goat wearing a nurse's cap was standing next to me.

Ironically, I knew I wasn't dreaming because of the goat. His name is Totes, and whenever things get *weird*, he shows up. His superpower transformed him into a goat, but he's never been able to turn himself back into a human.

Some superpowers just suck.

"What's with the hat?" I asked with a raspy voice.

"It's part of the uniform."

"So you're the school nurse now?"

"Nope."

The clock on the wall said eight p.m. Kepler's memorial service was at noon, which meant . . .

"I've been *asleep* for *eight* hours?" I said.

"Not *asleep*," Totes said. "Unconscious. *Huge* difference. Honestly, as many times as you've been knocked out, you should probably get your brain scanned to make sure all your stuff is working right."

"What happened?" I asked. "The last thing I remember is Donnie, and . . . Dexter. Dexter was gonna hurt Donnie! What happened to Donnie?"

Totes shrugged. "I don't know about any Donnie, but Dexter's fine. He woke up around six and got some dinner. He's been eating ever since—that boy can *pack it in*."

"So is everybody gone? Did they all go home?"

Noah and Penny appeared in the doorway.

"Not *everybody*," Noah said. "I'm here for the summer, remember?"

Noah wasn't allowed to leave because of the fire on his head. Students who couldn't control their powers had to live at the school full-time.

Penny didn't have that problem, though.

"But you could've gone home," I said to her.

"I didn't really have anything better to do, y'know?" she said. "Anything to get out of a long car ride, am I right?"

Totes leaned in. "She *refused* to leave. Said she wasn't goin' anywhere until you woke up and she *knew* you were okay."

Penny blushed.

Pretty sure I did, too.

AWWW, THEY GOT THEM **LOVE** SWEATS!

EW.

"Whatever, okay?" Penny said. "I'd never just *leave* you like that. I'm not *Victoria*."

"What happened to Vic?" I asked.

"Nothing," Totes said. "She just went home. Dexter asked about her when he woke up, but she was already gone. He was pretty bummed about it." He paused. "Maybe *that's* why he's eating so much. . . ."

"Huh," I said.

Feeling sorry for Dexter was weird.

That's when I noticed Jordan wasn't there, either.

Or, if he was, he was invisible . . . and naked.

"Wait, where's Jordan?" I asked.

"Oh, he peaced out, too," Penny said. "I tried telling him to stay. . . ."

I wasn't surprised. That's Jordan—living in his own world, doing his own "Jordan" things. Sometimes our worlds collided. Sometimes they didn't.

It wasn't a big deal.

The ghost of Professor Duncan floated through the wall. He smiled, happy to see me. "Ben! Welcome back! Sorry about almost killing you back there. We'll monitor you until the morning, and then you're free to go home."

"What happened?" I asked, still feeling sore.

"You were shocked," Duncan said.

"I saw one of your discs land on Donnie's neck," I said. "But who threw it?"

"You know who that kid is?" Duncan asked quietly.

"Yeah, I do, but do you?" I said.

Duncan nodded.

"Who threw the disc?" I asked again.

"Headmaster Archer," Duncan said. "After Donnie appeared, he ran inside to grab one."

"You mean it wasn't an accident?" Noah said. "He *meant* to electrocute Donnie? Why?"

"That's classified," Duncan said.

"C'mon," Penny said. "We already know *everything* about that kid."

Duncan took a deep breath and then peeked out the door to make sure nobody else was around. "Fine," he said. "Unfortunately, yes, Archer and I have been under strict orders to use whatever force necessary to catch Donnie if he ever showed up."

Noah cocked his head. "Is he dangerous?"

"*He's* not," Duncan said, "but what he's doing *is*— skipping forward through time. According to the history books, Donnie went missing in 1963. That means he *never* went back home. If he *does* return to 1963, then his actions will alter our current timeline, and history will be changed yet again."

I chewed my lip. "A small change back then could mean a whole different world now."

"Precisely," Duncan said. "So the simplest solution is to prevent him from going back."

"By keeping him prisoner," Penny added.

"How can you even stop him from using his power?" I asked.

Wherever they were keeping Donnie couldn't have been good. I've never really heard of a *nice* way to keep somebody trapped. Even the Reaper was a prisoner outside the—oh no—*the Reaper.*

I totally forgot!

"What happened to the Reaper?" I said, frantic. "Did anyone catch him yet?"

Penny and Noah looked at each other like, *"What?"*

Duncan narrowed his eyes. "Excuse me?"

"The Reaper!" I said. "Donnie was wrestling with him when he appeared!"

"Donnie didn't appear to be under any stress on the stage," Duncan said.

"Are you kidding me? He was screaming for help!" I said. "He was all, 'Get it off me, get it off!' "

"His *mask*," Duncan said. "He was talking about his *Elvis mask.*"

"Nooo, he *wasn't* talking about the mask!" I said. "The Reaper was on his head, trying to connect with him!"

"How do you know all this?" Duncan said, suddenly *very* concerned.

At that moment, a terrible noise pierced my ears. It was like thunder had cracked right next to my face.

Penny, Noah, and Totes covered their ears. Even Duncan was trying to block the sound, but how does a ghost cover his ears?

The thunder grew louder, transforming into a violent whooshing sound until suddenly . . . it stopped.

Dead silence is a creepy thing.

But it didn't last long.

That's when Kepler Academy shook like a bomb had gone off outside. The walls split as glass shattered and wood splintered.

We all looked at one another, none of us sure what exactly was happening, but I knew we were all thinking the same thing.

The Reaper was back.

And he was *not* happy.

CHAPTER FIVE

We ran down the hall, but it's not so easy when the ground keeps moving underneath you.

As we passed the kitchen, I saw Dexter lying trapped under a fallen metal table on the floor, food splattered all over him. His eyes were closed. His lights were completely out.

I had to help him.

I'm not a fan of the kid, but I didn't want him to die.

Ceiling tiles fell as I stumbled toward him. When Penny, Noah, and Totes saw what I was doing, they didn't hesitate to help. Good thing, too, because I wasn't strong enough to lift Dexter by myself.

That kid's a beast.

Totes put his head under the metal table and lifted it so Penny, Noah, and I could slide Dexter out.

The three of us hoisted him onto Totes and ran back to the hallway to get the heck out of the school.

The building was still shaking when we reached the

lobby, so Duncan went ahead of us to make sure it was safe.

It wasn't.

Headmaster Archer and a handful of teachers were in the lobby, too.

"You kids need to take cover!" Duncan said to us. He pointed at the coffee shop. "Get behind the counter and stay hidden!"

"Stay hidden? What's going on?" I said. *"Is it the Reaper?"*

Duncan shook his head. "No, it's *not* the Reaper! Now stay low, and hurry!"

We scooted along the ground until we got to the coffee shop, and then one by one, we climbed over the counter.

The earth rumbled as we huddled together, hiding from whatever Duncan had seen. If it wasn't the Reaper attacking the school, then what was even happening?

Duncan floated above us, staring in awe.

I couldn't help myself.

I peeked over the counter.

The night sky was an eerie yellow, and the entire front of the school was *gone*, ripped to pieces, getting sucked into a giant vortex of doom hovering overhead.

In front of the school stood the source of the vortex—a younger-lookin' dude, wearing an outfit that would make Star-Lord jealous, circling his hands to control that *thing* in the sky.

I can't lie—he looked *super* cool.

Behind him were a woman wearing a similar out-fit and a giant lizard wearing nothing at all. It was the first time I'd ever seen a supervillain team in real life.

The leader clasped his hands shut, and the vortex dissipated. The shaking stopped, and the dust settled as the three supervillains walked into the lobby.

Archer stood his ground, but the rest of the teachers bailed. The bad guys didn't even bother chasing them.

"Is it him?" Penny asked. "Is it the Reaper?"

"No," I said, somehow relieved, even though three *new* screwballs were threatening our lives.

Archer said nothing.

"Really? The silent treatment is gonna get you no-where," the leader taunted.

Archer wasn't in the mood for games. "What do you want, William?"

"You remember me!" William said with a giddy hop.

"Of course I do," Archer said, stiff-faced. "You grad-uated only *four* years ago."

William walked around the lobby, scooting rubble aside with every step. "Has it been only four years? *Feels* longer." He held his hand out to the woman. "You remember Delilah?"

Archer nodded.

"But do you know who *this* is?" William asked, running up to the lizard and patting him on his scaly chest. "Take *one* guess. If you get it right, we'll leave. No harm, no foul. Except for tearing the front of the school apart."

Archer shook his head, confused.

William grabbed the lizard's jaw and squeezed his scaly lips together. "C'mon . . . he was quiet. Kinda dorky. No friends. Probably because he stinks like a turtle."

Those were some pretty harsh clues, but Archer still had no idea.

"It's Matthew!" William said. "Matthew Alexo . . . Alexou . . . Alexa . . ." He sighed. "Delilah, how do you say his last name?"

"Alexopoulos," she said.

William snapped his fingers. "Yes, that."

Archer's face softened. "Matthew?"

The lizard snapped his jaw at William, lightning fast, but William yanked his hand back before it got chomped off.

Matthew looked away with a snarl.

Penny looked at Totes. "Do you know those guys?"

Totes nodded. "Yeah, I remember him. William Wolff. He was a total wad when he went here. Doesn't look like he grew out of it."

"What's his power?" I asked.

"He creates funnels of dark energy that suck every-thing into it," Duncan said from above us.

"What about the woman?" Penny said.

"That's Delilah Spring," Totes said. "She gener-ates electricity or something . . . I don't know. And then Matthew—his skin had scales when he was here, but he never went full Geico gecko on us. That must've hap-pened *after* he graduated."

"Poor Matthew," Duncan whispered sadly.

"*What* do you want?" Archer said again.

"We want the *kid*," William said immediately.

"Me?" I whispered. "But why would they want *me*?"

Noah rolled his eyes. "Pretty sure he's talking about Donnie. Not everything's about you, bro."

Oh right, why *would* they want me?

I'm a nobody.

"So where is he?" William demanded.

Archer didn't skip a beat. "I don't know who you're talking about. Everyone left for the summer."

"Look, I don't want to be here longer than I have to be, so just tell us where Donald Kepler is. Please?"

"Haven't you heard?" Archer said, unfazed. "The old headmaster's dead. We had a service for him earlier today. There's leftover hot dogs if you're hungry."

"Uck." William made a face. "Funeral food. No thanks."

Delilah's eyes flashed and glowed bright white. "We're wasting time! Give me a minute alone with this old fossil. Let me light him up."

William raised his fist. "No! I *got* this, okay?"

Delilah scowled but didn't argue.

"Mr. Archer," William said, stepping over debris. "You know who sent us here, right?"

"The Abandoned Children," Archer said coldly.

My heart dropped.

I've heard of them before.

The Abandoned Children are a group of descendants who believe Kepler Academy abandons and ignores students once they graduate.

William continued. "So if we really wanted to mess this place up, then we *all* would've come, and trust me, there's *a lot* of us now. But that's *not* what we want. The vote was close, but most of us were in favor of *keeping* this place around."

"We *know* he's here," Delilah said.

"Is that right?" Archer said sarcastically. "And just how do you know that?"

William clapped his hands, beckoning someone still outside. "Come on in, darling, don't be shy!"

Footsteps crunched as the fourth member of their supervillain team stepped up.

INTRODUCING...
LADY VICTORIA!!
MWAAAAAA!!!

Victoria had joined the Abandoned Children.

Vic scowled at the headmaster, her arms folded. "I know it was *Donnie*," she said. "He told us his name and then said he *hated* our hot dogs, but our hot dogs are *awesome!*"

The smiling William turned to Vic. "The hot dog thing doesn't matter, sweetie, but it's okay—you're new. For future reference, be as simple and clear as possible. Avoid frivolities."

Vic nodded. "Sir."

William cringed. "And *don't* call me sir. It sounds so *gross*." He turned back to Archer. "So there it is. We want your time traveler. Simple as that. Easy peasy pumpkin pie."

"Lemon squeezy," the giant lizard corrected.

"Shut up, Matthew!" William snapped, clenching his fists like a toddler. "You're only here because you're a cool reptile, but nobody actually likes you!"

I leaned into Noah. "A time-traveling kid *would be* pretty dope to a team of supervillains."

"Right?" Noah said.

Duncan motioned for us to huddle up. "Okay," he said. "William wants Donnie, and it's only a matter of time before he tears this school apart to find him."

"Not if we stop him," Noah said.

By *we*, Noah meant him and Penny.

I wasn't included in that, but y'know what? I was

cool with it. It had been a long day, and I just wanted to go home.

Penny shook her head. "I'm *not* using my power. I'd end up blowing this whole mountain to kingdom come."

"A fight isn't the answer," Duncan said, peering over the countertop again. "If you all teamed up against Matthew, you *might* have a chance, but there's no contest against William or Delilah. They're two of the most powerful students I've ever known."

"We're pretty powerful, too," Noah said.

"Not like them," Duncan said. "If anything, those two are *overpowered*, as in, *overwhelmingly* powerful. And they won't let you come back for round two. They *will* kill you."

"So what do we do?" Noah asked.

"We need to get Donnie out of here," Duncan said.

"That's great," I said. "You guys do that. I'll just hang out here until this all blows over."

"They'll find you," Noah said.

"Nah," I said. "I'll run into the forest or something."

"So that's it? You're not gonna help?" Noah asked.

"I'll just hold you back," I said. "What can I do?"

"You're the most important one here," Duncan said.

"Nooo," I said, blushing. "I don't even have a power. *You guys* are the ones who can—"

"We need your biometrics," Duncan said. "Donnie's in the lab."

"Oh," I said as Penny hid a chuckle.

Last year, I got to work in Duncan's lab. My biometrics were used to unlock the door—it's like using your DNA as the key.

"But you never deleted my biometric data," I said, trying to save face. "Which means you *wanted* me to get back in there someday, right? Like, to redeem myself?"

"False." Duncan wiggled his fingers at me. "I would've deleted them long ago if I could actually touch a keyboard."

"Whatever. That means Donnie's safe," I said. "They can't get in there."

"The lab isn't impenetrable," Duncan said. "They'll break into it eventually."

Guess I wasn't going home as soon as I thought.

Pebbles suddenly pelted our heads, like the walls were throwing rocks at us.

"Ow!" Penny said, rubbing her noggin. "Whatever we do, we need to hurry before this whole place caves in."

"There's an exit behind the coffee shop," Duncan said. "William and his friends are distracted by Archer, so you can . . . sneak . . . What in the . . . ?"

He stared past the lobby, his attention caught by something outside the broken building.

"What is it? Are there other Abandoned Children?" Penny whispered. "Is it the Reaper?"

The ghost's eyes narrowed. "Go on without me, kids. I think this whole thing is much *bigger* than we understand."

He didn't wait for us to say anything. He just floated into the floor and disappeared.

"How can he just leave us like that?" Penny said, taking quick breaths and squeezing the palms of her hands. "Wouldn't he wanna make sure we got out in one piece?"

Penny's skin was lit, but not the cool kind of lit, like, "*Yo, that party was LIT!*" Her skin was literally glowing.

"What's going on with you?" I asked.

She nodded quickly. "Nothing, I'm fine," she said, even though she very obviously wasn't.

She was scared. *Really* scared.

I put my hand on her ankle. It definitely helped, because she relaxed enough that the glow died down.

"I'm good," she sighed. "I'm all good."

I hate to say it, but I didn't believe her.

Dexter groaned from the floor, his eyes half open. "What . . . what happened?" he asked a little too loudly.

"Shhhhut your mouth hole!" I whispered.

"What? Why?" Dexter asked, sitting up. "What's going on? Am I in Cool Beanz?"

"Yes!" Noah said quietly. "The school was attacked, and we're hiding here!"

"Attacked? By who?" Dexter asked, scratching the back of his neck as he looked out at the lobby. He stopped abruptly. "Is that Victoria?"

Dexter's eyes went from the lobby, to us, and then back to the lobby as his brain churned away in that Neanderthal head of his.

He didn't have a clue what was happening. All he knew was that his best friend was on the opposite side of where we were.

Dexter and I made eye contact for a split second.

I wanted to plead with him. To tell him to get down because *those* were the bad guys out there.

But I was too late.

CHAPTER SIX

"**T**hey're back here!" Dexter shouted, slapping his fat hands over and over on the counter.

Totes took matters into his own hooves, ramming Dexter so hard that the kid went flying.

"What's the plan?" Noah said.

But I was already gone, running toward the back of the coffee shop.

"Go! I'll hold them back!" Totes shouted.

"I love that goat," Penny said, "but he needs a better battle cry."

I burst into the hallway, where I could hear the sounds of a *bazonkers* Power Battle coming from the lobby.

"Dude, seriously," Noah said to me as he and Penny caught up. "You gotta stop taking off like that!"

"I don't have a power," I reminded my friend. "You guys can defend yourselves, but I'm a sitting duck out there!"

"But that's not teamwork!" Noah said, angry.

"Fight about it later!" Penny said. "Right now, we need to get to the lab!"

The three of us started running. As long as the Abandoned Children were busy in the lobby, we'd be fine. Or so we thought . . . until the giant lizard-dude burst through the wall next to us.

We bolted, going all out like we were racing in some kind of horrific version of the Olympics where a giant dragon chows down on the losers.

Noah lit a trail of fire behind us, setting the whole floor ablaze. Too bad it didn't slow Matthew down. He bounced off the wall and onto the ceiling, where he continued chasing us upside down.

The door to the west wing was at the end of the hall. As soon as Penny and Noah pushed through it, I got an idea. I hid behind the open door, and when Matthew caught up to us, I slammed it shut in his stupid lizard face.

It would've been *awesome* if it had worked.

But it didn't.

Not even a little.

He tore through the door like it was paper, sending me rolling on the floor.

Noah shot fireballs from his hands, but Matthew's skin was thick. The fireballs didn't even slow him down. He smashed Noah against the wall so hard it cracked. Then the lizard scooped Penny up with his tail.

A burst of yellow energy flared from Penny's body,

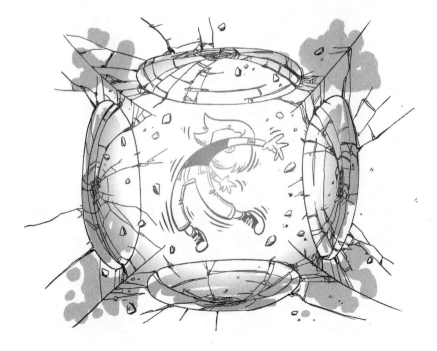

pushing the walls out like a balloon. Matthew was launched backward through the door.

Penny dropped to the ground, her skin glowing as she scrubbed her forearms. *"Please, no, no, no!"* she repeated.

Penny's power was coming out *without* her uke.

And without her control.

It was the same problem Angel had before she almost exploded.

I tried to help her up, but she pulled away.

"I'm FINE!" she said. "We gotta go!"

I was more worried about Penny than Matthew, but she was right. We had to get to Donnie before the Abandoned Children found him.

The three of us ran down the steps and into the secret tunnel under the school. It was dark and dank and smelled like something had died down there.

Noah's fiery hairdo lit our path as we jogged to the end of the tunnel, our footsteps echoing through the shadows. The lab door scanned my face, slid open, and then sealed shut behind us.

The walls of Duncan's lab came to life with lights and holographic displays. The last time I was there, the table in the center of the room was filled with gadgets and gizmos, but those were gone. Now, the only thing on the table was Donnie Kepler.

He was laid out, his eyes rolled back. Headmaster Kepler's weird lightbulb helmet sat on his head.

Donnie sat up, swaying like Jell-O. *"Well, hello, sweet cheeks!"* he slurred as he bopped Penny on the nose. *"How's about we share a milkshake sometime?"*

"First—ew!" Penny said. "Second—what the heck's wrong with him? Is that the same hat Headmaster Kepler had all year?"

"Yeah, but I don't know what it does," I said.

Donnie gave Noah a wonky smile. *"Whoa, your head's on fire, buddy! Better put it out!"*

"Does it make him drunk?" Noah asked.

"I think it keeps him from using his power or something," I said.

Just then, Matthew slammed against the entrance,

rattling the whole room. We spun around as the slams came again and again.

"It's a lizard monster that wants to capture you," Noah said.

"*Whaaaat . . . ?*" Donnie said. "*You guys got lizard monsters in the future? Oh, that's cooool. . . .*" He slid off the table and hobbled toward the door. "*I wanna see it!*"

"No!" I shouted, holding him back.

The door slid up a few inches with the next slam. Matthew bent over and peered inside, his eye scanning the room like that velociraptor from *Jurassic Park*.

Nobody moved.

Nobody even breathed.

It was like time had stopped, and I got this glimmer of hope that maybe Matthew thought we were gone. It was possible that we *weren't* gonna die in there!

At least until Donnie opened his big mouth. *"Lizard monster!"*

Matthew gripped the bottom edge of the door and started pulling up, slowly scraping it open.

"Is there another way out?" Penny said.

"Nope, that's it," I said.

"Then we're done," Noah said. "Game over."

"Are we playing a game?" Donnie asked.

As the crack widened, Matthew pushed his tail under it and slid the door further upward.

"I played a game," Donnie said. *"Hide-and-seek. And I WON."*

"Can you shut him up?" Penny asked.

"No, wait," I said as a wrinkle formed in my brain. "We can use Donnie's power to get us out of here! Just make sure you're touching him when he does it!"

Noah and I tore the contraption off Donnie's head.

His eyes squeezed shut as he sucked air through his teeth. He pressed his fingers against his forehead like he had the worst migraine in the history of all migraines ever.

KA-CHUNK!

The door finally buckled, sliding open all the way, and Matthew entered the room.

Donnie opened his eyes and screamed. *"WHAT IS THAT THING?"*

Penny held on to Donnie's wrist, Noah touched his head, and I grabbed his shoulders.

GET US OUT OF HERE!!

The lizard dove for us.

And then everything disappeared.

CHAPTER SEVEN

The four of us splashed down in an inch of water.

I glanced over my shoulder to make sure Matthew was gone.

He was.

I got to my knees, staring in awe at the entire universe that was under me. The stars. The galaxies.

It was all so beautiful.

Everything above the water was black. Blacker than black. It didn't exist. It was nothing. And it went on for eternity. This was the Outside—the last place I had seen Headmaster Kepler. But if he was still out there, he wasn't anywhere nearby.

I hoped he was okay.

Penny and Noah stared at the stars through the water.

"Is this it?" Penny whispered. "Are we . . . outside the universe?"

She and Noah beamed with smiles when I nodded.

And if we could've admired it a little longer, we would have, but that's when Donnie started hightailing it out of there.

"Get away from me!" he shouted at us.

"We can't let him go back without us or we'll be stuck here!" I said.

We ran after Donnie, splashing water with each step. He was about half a football field away when he slowed down to peer into different spots in the water.

"What's he doing?" Penny said.

"Looking for a place to drop back in!" I said. "The reflections show us the past and the future!"

"This is crazy!" Noah shouted. "I can see my fifth birthday!"

"Hey, there's the time I accidentally set fire to the living room rug!" Penny said.

The farther I ran, the younger I got in the reflections, until I ran past the day I was born. After that, there was nothing but clear water.

Donnie looked back at us with fear in his eyes.

"Donnie, wait!" I said. "We're the good guys!"

"Nice try!" he shouted as he hobbled to a stop, searching the ground. Then he sank into the water.

I slid like I was stealing home and reached my hand into the water ripples Donnie made, gripping the neck of his shirt.

Noah and Penny dove across the water and grabbed

my ankles just in time, and we all suddenly fell into the middle of a dark forest.

The stars were overhead, where they belonged, which was a good sign. It meant that we were back inside the universe and that it was nighttime.

Donnie's shirt was still in my hand, but Donnie wasn't in it.

I must've ripped it right off him.

"Where are we?" Penny asked.

"Looks like we're in the forest," Noah said.

Penny glared at Noah. "Are you sure?"

"Yeah, I'm . . . oh, you're being sarcastic," Noah said.

"Where'd he go?" I said, looking around.

"He couldn't have gotten far," Penny said.

"Shhh," I said, finger to my lips. "You hear anything?"

Noah and Penny fell silent. They shook their heads at the same time.

"We'd hear his footsteps if he was running," I said. "So he's either *hiding*, or he went *back* Outside."

"And if he went back Outside, then we're stuck here," Penny said. "Wherever *here* is."

Noah's hair-on-fire took some of the edge off the darkness. He just needed to be careful of all the dead pine needles at our feet. Wouldn't want the whole forest to burst into flames.

Penny cupped her hands around her mouth. *"Donnie Kepler! Come out, come out, wherever you are!"*

"Do you *want* it to sound like we're *hunting* him?" Noah asked.

"But . . . we *are*," Penny said.

"Right, but . . . *still*," Noah said.

All of a sudden, branches cracked to our right. As soon as our heads snapped toward the sound, Donnie's shadowy figure bolted, and the chase was on again.

"Stop!" I shouted as tree leaves slapped my face.

Donnie didn't respond. Obviously, he was too busy running for his life.

Noah had to slow down once he realized his fire kept toasting low-hanging branches. "Guys, I gotta stop!"

Penny was ahead of me, tearing through the forest like some kind of tree ninja.

Without Noah lighting the way, it was harder to see her or Donnie. Actually, it was harder to see *anything*.

Just for the record, my pain tolerance is pretty low, but on a scale from one to ten, I'd say that face-planting a tree trunk at full speed is a record-breaking eleven.

Penny doubled back to help me just as Noah caught up to us. I held a finger under my bloody nose. "Where'd he go?"

Penny army-crawled to the edge of the forest. Just past that spot was an open field of freshly cut grass. "He's out there."

Noah and I shuffled up next to her and looked out.

Everything was familiar, but at the same time, it wasn't. We were looking down at a massive ski lodge.

Out-of-order ski lifts were in the yard behind the building, snaking their way up the mountain and disappearing over the peak.

Donnie was at the front door of the ski lodge, hugging a woman tightly.

"You see who he's hugging?" Penny asked.

Noah and I nodded together.

I had seen that woman's picture in the very first Kepler Academy yearbook. She was even wearing the same outfit from the photo. Her hair stood straight up over her head like she was the Bride of Frankenstein's prettier sister.

It was Mary Kepler—Donnie's mom.

We had traveled back in time.

It was 1963.

CHAPTER EIGHT

Penny, Noah, and I hid in the forest, watching Donnie hug his mom.

"Go get him," Penny said.

But I couldn't do it.

Donnie was holding his mom the same way I would've held my mom if I had just woken up from a nightmare.

Mary knelt by her son and listened as he spoke. I couldn't hear what he said, but he kept pointing right where we were hiding.

You see, the thing about Noah's flaming hair is that it makes it hard to play hide-and-seek.

"We're busted," Noah said.

"He wasn't supposed to come back!" Penny said. "We might've just screwed up the future!"

"This is what Headmaster Kepler was afraid of, wasn't it?" Noah asked.

"We just need Donnie to take us back," Penny said. "So somebody has to run out and grab him."

"We can't just *grab* him, though," Noah said. "He'll put up a fight. His mom will *totally* set off the alarms and all the students will come outside and it'll become this whole big thing that'll be known as *the incident* in 1963, which *will* affect the future."

All this time-travel stuff was making my brain cry.

"If we go out hard and fast, then they won't have time to understand what we're doing," Penny said.

"But then what?" I asked. "We can't *force* him to help us. We need to come at this differently."

We looked back at the academy.

Mary and Donnie were gone.

"Well, this just got harder," Penny said.

"What about *asking* him for help?" Noah suggested.

Penny shrugged. "That's not bad. We can just tell him what's up, and maybe even talk to a teacher or something."

"It's 1963, so Headmaster Kepler is in charge," Noah said. "We'd be in a *metric ton* of trouble, but he'd definitely help us. Maybe he'd even take us back himself."

My heart sank at the thought of seeing Kepler.

"No way," I said. "We should stay *far* away from him while we're here."

"Why?" Penny asked.

I thought about it, but I didn't have an answer.

Honestly, I wasn't sure why I didn't want to see him. It was just something about having to talk to him while knowing his future. Knowing where he was gonna end up. Knowing that he'd get fried in an explosion and then trapped outside of the universe for eternity all because of . . . me.

Oh.

Guilt.

That's why I didn't want to see him.

"Fine. Let's talk to Donnie's mom, then," Noah said. "She looked nice."

"Okay, but who's gonna go first?" Penny asked.

"Seriously?" Noah said, shaking his head. He stepped out of the forest. "So immature."

Penny and I followed at a safe distance behind our friend as he walked to the Lodge.

"The first fourteen descendants are in there," I said.

I don't think Penny cared. "Yup," was all she said.

"Abigail's in there," I added.

Abigail was the villain from our first year. She ran the school's security but went ballistic when she figured out Headmaster Kepler had changed history.

I still don't know *how* she figured that out, though.

In Kepler's original timeline, Abigail was a legit superhero with maxed-out stats and a killer costume, saving the world in style.

In our timeline, she was a low-level security guard.

Not like that's bad or anything, but you can imagine how *peeved* she was when she discovered what she *could've* been. Kepler had thwarted her destiny.

But all that was gonna happen in the future.

At *this* moment, she was just a happy-go-lucky kid.

I don't know why, but I felt incredibly sorry for her.

"It's cool," Noah said. "We'll just go inside and talk to whoever's at the front desk. You see, Ben? This is what a *plan* looks like. You might wanna take some notes."

I made a face. "They're gonna freak when they see your head on fire. There are only fifteen kids in the world with superpowers in 1963, and they're all inside that lodge."

"Wait," Penny said. "We might not have to go inside."

Mary walked out the front doors alone. She moved like royalty, with perfect posture, long strides, and her arms behind her back. The way she was headed for us was intense. Intimidating. Scary.

Noah stopped in his tracks. Penny and I did, too.

"Ah, hello, Mrs. Kepler!" Noah chirped as friendly as possible. He sounded corny as heck and absolutely guilty.

Mary didn't say anything.

"My name is Noah Nichols, and these are my friends, Penny and—"

Noah couldn't finish his sentence, though, because that's when Mary planted her feet and swung a gigantic crossbow out from behind her back.

"Ohhhhh no," Noah said.

She pulled the trigger. The crossbow fired loudly, sounding like something from the Middle Ages.

KER-CHCK!

A glowing net shot out, covering Noah and tightening around his body as he fell flat on his back. He was tied up, but whatever she did extinguished the fire that had been on his head for the past couple of months.

Mary pulled another arrow back on the crossbow, fixing her eyes on Penny and me. She hoisted it up, aiming at Penny, whose skin was radiating energy again.

Penny stumbled back, covering her face. I could feel the warmth simmering from her body. She was losing control again.

"No, don't!" Penny pleaded. "I'm not doing this on purpose!"

But as soon as Mary fired the weapon, the net wrapped Penny up like a human burrito, and the glow disappeared from her skin.

Both of my friends were on the ground, trying to tell Mary they weren't the bad guys, but she wasn't listening.

She was reloading.

I laughed nervously with my hands up. "I'm good! I'll go quietly! I give up! Seriously, if I had a white flag, I'd be waving it *so hard* right now!"

Mary pointed the crossbow at me.

"Please?" I said.

She paused for a second.

There was a fire in her eyes—the kind that said, *"Don't mess with my kid."*

And then she pulled the trigger.

CHAPTER NINE

About half an hour later, the three of us were sitting in a cabin in the woods. In the future, it was the crummy cabin where Totes and his friends lived. In 1963, it was home to the Keplers.

Donnie's dad, Richard Kepler, was in the chair across from us, petting the crossbow in his lap like it was an animal.

Mary leaned against the kitchen counter, and

Donnie, wearing a fresh T-shirt, sat in the chair next to his dad.

"I must apologize for my wife," Richard said. "She *loves* this crossbow. I made it myself. I call it the Power Dampener. Do you know why?"

"Because it dampens powers?" Penny said.

Richard pointed at Penny. "Because it dampens powers. It basically shuts them off."

"We noticed," Noah said, playing with his newly normal hair.

"Funny thing about this weapon, though," Richard said. "It only works on people with *powers*. If your hair was on fire, say, because you were wearing a special helmet, then it *wouldn't* have worked on you."

"But it did work," Noah said.

"But it did work," Richard repeated, nodding slowly. "And *that's* something of a mystery. There are only fifteen children on the planet with superpowers, and those fifteen are the offspring of seven *specific* people. We know who those seven are, and who their children are. But we don't know who *you* are, so the sixty-four-thousand-dollar question is . . . who *are* you?"

Nobody answered.

"Why were you chasing my son?" Mary asked from the kitchen.

Again, nobody answered.

We couldn't.

It was too risky.

Anything we said could screw up the future.

Richard turned to Donnie. "Why were you in the forest, son?"

That time, it was Donnie who said nothing.

And then I understood. Richard and Mary really had no clue what was happening. Donnie might've gotten us caught, but he hadn't explained *any of it* to his parents.

He was afraid of getting in trouble.

"*That does it!*" Richard shouted suddenly, spit flying. "*Who are you? What are you doing here? What's your mission? Why were you chasing after my son, and how did you know about the ski lodge? Tell me the truth! We have ways of making you talk!*"

Penny absolutely snapped.

WHAT'RE **YOU** DOING HERE? WHO SENT **YOU**?? **YOU** LIKE YELLING AT A BUNCH OF KIDS?? HUH?? DO YA??

Richard sat back, speechless, clearly shocked at getting roasted by a twelve-year-old. He stared daggers at my friend, his eye twitching and everything. Everyone else waited for him to blow. He was a stick of dynamite, and Penny had just lit the fuse.

But that's when Mary roared with laughter. "I *like* you," she said to Penny. "I don't think I've ever heard *anyone* talk to my husband like that before!"

Richard groaned.

"We weren't trying to hurt your son," I blurted out.

"Yes," Mary said softly. "I realized that once I got a better look at the three of you. You'll have to forgive me for being rather aggressive. In the dark, you looked menacing, and the way Donnie begged for help, *my goodness*, I was expecting *werewolves* to run out of the forest."

Richard folded his arms and huffed loudly like he wanted his wife to side with him.

"They're *children*," Mary protested.

At that, Richard sighed, finally letting up, like, "*Fine, you win.*"

Mary came around the couch and sat on the armrest. "Now," she said. "What are your names?"

"Noah Nichols."

"Penny Plum."

"Ben Braver."

Mary tapped the top of Noah's head. "You clearly have a superpower—"

"But you're *not* a student," Richard interrupted.

"Is it possible one of the seven had a child we don't know about?" Mary asked her husband.

"Improbable," Richard said. "But not impossible."

I finally caved. It would've been a waste of time to listen to them try to figure out what our deal was, so I straight up told them. "We're from the future."

"Ah-ha," Mary said. "Our son brought you here."

Donnie shut his eyes and waited for the scolding of a lifetime.

"What's the punishment for bringing guests from the future?" Richard asked. "Should that be *one* or *two* spanks?"

Donnie's eyes shot open, and he stared into space like a deer caught in headlights.

DID YOU SAY SPANKS?

"You know I'm joking!" he said heartily, slapping his son's knee.

Donnie slumped back, relieved.

Mary clapped her hands and strolled into the kitchen. "Enough of this," she said. "Everybody follow me."

". . . Why?" I asked cautiously.

Richard stood from his chair and loomed over the three of us on the couch. His eyes narrowed as a smile stretched out under his nose.

"Because," he said.

IT'S DINNER TIME.

CHAPTER TEN

Dinner was *out of this world.*

On the menu was chicken à la king—diced chicken mixed with vegetables in a creamy sauce like gravy, and then poured over some biscuits—just like my mom makes.

Richard poured everybody a glass of milk and took a seat at the end of the table, across from Mary at the other end.

As Donnie told the story of what happened to him, we all filled our plates. Penny's a vegetarian but didn't want to be rude, so she scooped only vegetables onto hers.

". . . and then I woke up in some kind of mad scientist's laboratory," Donnie said. "That's when I wigged out and came back here."

I shoved a forkful of food into my mouth. "Yeah, I grabbed his shirt right when he used his power. That's how we followed him."

"That was my *favorite* shirt," Donnie pouted.

"Sorry," I said.

"Fascinating," Richard said. "I didn't realize you could take people *with* you out there."

"Ditto," Donnie said.

"But why did you panic?" Mary asked.

"What?" Donnie said.

Mary dabbed the corners of her mouth with a napkin. "You said you . . . *wigged out.*"

"Oh, right, yeah, because of the giant lizard monster in the room," Donnie said. "I forgot to mention that."

"Uh, no," I said. "There's only one. At least I *think* there's only one. And he's not exactly a monster, he's actually a descendant. The school was attacked—"

"Kepler Academy was attacked?" Richard said.

"Yeah, by some bad guys called the Abandoned Children," I said. "They wanted Donnie."

"How did they know he was there?" Richard asked.

"Well, he showed up during . . ." I stopped, not wanting to say that *he showed up to his own funeral* because that's kinda messed up. "Uh, Donnie made a pretty big scene."

"But why would they want our son?" Mary asked.

Richard was on the same page as me. "A time traveler would be helpful to *any* organization," he said.

"Right?" I said. "So we need to get back and stop them."

"Their attack on the school is nothing to worry about anymore," Richard stated bluntly.

"What?" I asked. "Why not?"

"Because Donnie's safe with us here in 1963," Richard said.

"But they'll still attack," Noah said.

"They'll lose interest when they realize he's gone," Richard said firmly.

I think he was only worried about his son, and since the Abandoned Children had no way to travel back in time, Donnie was safe, and that was that.

Hopefully, they *would* lose interest after realizing Donnie was gone, but I seriously doubted it.

Mary set her fork down next to her plate. She looked at her son, perplexed. "What were you doing in a laboratory?"

Donnie shrugged. "I dunno. I just woke up in it. I don't even know how I got there."

Mary turned to me. She didn't say anything, but it was obvious she was waiting for me to answer her question.

I didn't know what to say, because saying, *"The school was going to keep your kid prisoner inside a laboratory for the rest of his life so he couldn't use his power ever again"* would've been *kinda* rude.

That, and I was legit afraid of that woman.

Noah had that look in his eye, like he didn't want me to say something stupid. And Penny had that look in *her* eye like she was just *waiting* for me to say something stupid.

Lucky for me, I was saved by a knock at the door.

It wasn't my house, but I was the one who jumped up from the table to answer it. I didn't care—I just needed to get away from Mary's question.

I ran across the living room and twisted the doorknob on the heavy wooden door, swinging it wide open.

Penny and Noah gasped. Pretty sure I would've, too, but I could hardly breathe as I stared at the face of the man on the other side.

The man who started the academy.
The same man who saved my life.
It was Headmaster Kepler.
And he'd brought pie.

CHAPTER ELEVEN

I wasn't sure how long I was staring at the headmaster, but it was long enough that it got awkward. He was younger, with short hair and normal eyebrows—the headmaster in 1963. He had traveled back in time to save the world, but never returned to his timeline. That's how he was there.

I let him in even though it wasn't my house.

There he was—the man who was gonna die someday to save *my* life. I needed to warn him, right? To tell him what was gonna happen to him so that it *didn't* happen.

But I could barely talk.

"I'd be lying if I said I was pleased to meet you, after what I've already been told," Headmaster Kepler said, "but I'm also not one to be rude, so . . ."

He held out his hand to me.

"Donald Kepler," he said as we shook. "And who might you be?"

"I, uh, my name?" I gulped. "Ben Braver."

Kepler nodded, blew right past me, set his pie on the kitchen counter, and then went straight for the dinner table, where Noah and Penny introduced themselves, too. "How exciting," he said, eyeballing Donnie. Then with the most sarcastic tone I've ever heard, he said . . .

TIME TRAVELERS...

Donnie looked away.

The headmaster clearly wasn't in a fabulous mood.

Kepler scooped food onto his plate, then he pointed his fork at Noah. "Mother tells me your head was on fire."

Donnie and Headmaster Kepler were the same person, but different ages. I had to remind myself of that or else Headmaster Kepler calling Mary his mother was gonna get weird.

"Technically, it was my hair," Noah said. "I haven't been able to put it out for a really long time."

"Your Power Dampener worked!" Kepler said to Richard, then he turned back to Noah. "We've been testing that weapon on pig carcasses for six months now. Every carcass was completely vaporized by the net's dampening field being *too* strong."

"Wait, so how'd you know it wouldn't vaporize *me*?" Noah asked Mary.

"I didn't," she said, unruffled.

Whoa.

Mama bear was protective of her cub.

The headmaster reached his long arm across the table and grabbed a biscuit. "And what's *your* power?" he asked me.

"I don't have one, but I—"

He moved right along like I wasn't even there anymore. "And you, young miss?"

"I can make the energy in my body do things," Penny said.

"Curious," Kepler said. "What kinds of things?"

"Control animals. Or explode like an atom bomb."

"That's quite a wide range," Kepler said. "And what happens when you explode like an atom bomb?"

"Uh, I die?" she answered sarcastically.

Kepler paused in the middle of buttering his biscuit and raised an eyebrow. "How do you know you have that ability if you die?"

"Oh, it happened to a lady we knew," I said.

Mary gasped.

"No, I mean, it *almost* happened. Her brother turned her to stone to stop it, sooo . . ."

Richard and Kepler shared a look.

"Yup," I added.

"My power's too dangerous," Penny said, "so I swore I'd never use it again."

"At least not on purpose," I added quietly.

Penny glared at me, her skin radiating slightly. "What's *that* mean?" she snipped.

"C'mon, it's obvious!" I said. "Every time you spaz out, your skin glows! And what the heck even happened in that hallway with the lizard monster?"

Headmaster Kepler dropped his fork. *"There are lizard monsters in the future? When do they attack?"*

"It's not what you think," Richard said, disappointed.

Penny folded her arms. "Worry about yourself, Ben."

"It's for the best," Kepler said bluntly. "Powers aren't a blessing; they're a curse."

"Preach, preacher!" Penny exclaimed, closing her eyes and raising her hands.

"You can't be afraid of your powers forever," I said.

"Wanna bet?" Penny said.

"Ben's right," Richard said. "Fear *cannot* control you."

"And why not?" Kepler asked. "The child said she's a walking atom bomb!"

"Only if she's taught to fear herself," Mary said. "Anybody, powers or not, is at risk of exploding if they're taught nothing but fear their entire lives!"

"Fear *teaches* control," Kepler said.

"No," Richard said, leaning toward Penny. "You'll only learn to control your power when you *let go* of your fear, darling."

"*Yeah, right!*" Penny said super sarcastically. "I'm not ready to die yet, so forget *that*."

"All we're saying is that there's hope if you focus on the right thing," Richard said.

"*Pfft!* And what's the right thing?" Penny asked.

"Love," Mary said.

Penny and Kepler both laughed at that answer.

"Love versus fear!" Kepler said. "The endless debate."

"The academy will fail if we teach fear," Mary said like it was her millionth time.

"And the world will end if we don't," Kepler said like it was *his* millionth time. "I've seen it happen. And I stopped it from happening again!"

The room was so awkwardly silent that I could hear Kepler's teeth grind.

"Love versus fear?" I asked just to make noise. "Shouldn't it be love versus hate?"

"Hate comes from fear," Richard said. "People often grow to hate the things they fear."

I thought for a moment and then ran my mouth without thinking. "That's why you hate superpowers, isn't it?" I said to Kepler. "Because you're afraid of them."

The headmaster studied me with his beady, narrow eyes.

"Why are you even here?" he finally asked. "Noah and Penny, I understand, but why *you*?"

Ouch.

"Because he's a student at your school," Penny said, coming to my rescue. Good to know she had my back, even when we were fighting.

"But you don't have a power." Kepler continued to study me, deep in thought, probably wondering why he'd invite a normal dork to his school. "So there must be *something* special about you."

Double ouch.

"Is saving the school special enough for you?" Penny asked.

"*You* did that?" Kepler asked me.

Triple ouch.

"I mean, kind of, yeah," I said. "There was this woman named Abigail Cutter who went crazy and—"

"Little Abigail?" Mary said. "She's a student here."

"She grows up to become a villain," I said. "She was the school security guard until she found Headmaster Kepler's secret cave of secrets in the forest."

"That was *Abigail*?" Donnie gasped. He tried to play it off, but his dad saw right through him.

"*What* was Abigail?" Richard asked his son.

"Nothing," Donnie said. "I didn't say anything."

"What did you do?" the headmaster asked accusingly.

Donnie paused. "I kinda ran into her . . . in the future."

Richard rubbed his temples and groaned.

"I didn't mean to!" Donnie said. "I dropped in next to the forest, and she saw me. She chased me, but then we fell into that weird secret cave Ben was talking about. I went back Outside before she saw that it was me, so it's all good!"

Oh, man. I remember that *exact* night.

I couldn't believe it.

Neither could Penny.

She dove for Donnie across the table. "This is all *your* fault!" she screamed as Noah and I held her back.

"Abigail didn't even see me!" Donnie said.

"But she saw all those newspapers!" I said. "That's why she attacked the school! That's why she teamed up with Angel and Lindsay! *Every single thing that's happened started because you showed up that night!*"

"Fine, I'll just go back and fix it!" Donnie barked.

"*NO!*" Kepler boomed. "The future has *already* been affected by you."

"Right? *That's* why Donnie was in the lab," I said stupidly. "So he wouldn't mess anything else up!"

Noah and Penny froze.

"What did you say?" Mary asked softly.

Whoops.

"Nothing?" I said, repeating Donnie's words. "I didn't say anything."

Mary leaned forward. "*Why* was my son in the lab?"

I had already said it—no sense in dodging the question anymore. "Because he was a prisoner. I don't think you were gonna let him come back here," I said to Kepler.

"Why do you think that?" Kepler asked.

"Donnie went missing in 1963," I said. "If he was supposed to come back, then he'd be in the yearbooks, but . . . he's not."

"That means he can't stay," Richard whispered.

"I'm not going anywhere!" Donnie said, then he pointed a hard finger at Kepler. "You go Outside all the time! Why are the rules different for me?"

"Because I never drop into the future!" Kepler explained. "I simply observe it to keep it steady!"

Mary's face tightened, but tears welled in her eyes. She kicked her chair out and took her plate to the sink. "Well, it's preposterous to think our Donnie won't stay. He's *not* going back to the future."

"Mary . . ." Richard said with a shaky voice. "He *has* to go back."

Donnie sank in his seat but never argued.

"No!" Mary erupted. "He's *not* going back. He's staying even if we have to hide him for the rest of his life!"

Nobody said anything because Richard was right. If

Donnie disappeared in 1963, then he *had* to disappear in 1963 or else the future would change *again*.

Mary sobbed quietly.

Saddest. Dinner party. Ever.

CHAPTER TWELVE

Everybody at the table stared at nothing as Mary cried. Donnie had started tearing up, too, holding his knees and sniffling.

It was uncomfortable.

Like, *supes* uncomfortable.

Like, the kind of uncomfortable that made you wish your brain had a Delete button so you'd never have to remember how very uncomfortable it was.

And so, like the idiot I am, I tried to lighten the mood. "We need Donnie to come back anyway 'cause we could use his help to find the Reaper."

A record scratched somewhere in the distance. Pretty sure I even heard a small voice shout, *"Say whaaaat?"*

Richard and the headmaster snapped their heads toward me. Even Mary stopped crying.

The whole room was dead silent.

"The Reaper is *free*?" Richard asked.

Headmaster Kepler pounded his fist on the table and then pointed at Donnie. "You're going to undo everything I've worked for, you little brat!"

"What're you talking about?" Donnie said. "Who's the Reaper?"

"You don't know?" Penny asked. "That makes two of us. Or . . . four of us actually."

"Who is he?" I said. "A person? A monster? Some kind of invisible baby? He's really tiny, so it's possible that he's a baby!"

Kepler looked at Richard and Mary, who both nodded.

"If he's escaped, then the children need to know what they're up against," Richard said.

Kepler sighed, and then he explained EVERY-THING.

THE REAPER MAY NOT BE EXACTLY WHAT YOU THINK.

HE IS BETTER KNOWN AS...

Penny, Noah, and I were speechless.

"Sooo the Reaper is an *alien*," Penny finally said.

"A *squid* alien," Noah added. "And *he's* the reason people even have powers now."

"I did *not* see that coming," I said. "But why is he called the Reaper?"

"Newspapers gave him the name," Kepler said. "He's harmless by himself, but when connected with another human, he becomes extraordinarily powerful."

"Is that what happened to you?" I asked.

Kepler nodded. "Yes. He attached himself to me, not because I was special, but because I was simply in the wrong place at the wrong time."

"Did he overtake you? Is he that powerful?"

"Quite the opposite," Kepler said. "He's a weak creature without a host."

"But that means . . ."

Kepler nodded. "I . . . *allowed* our bond. I was a different man back then. . . . Our bond gave me new powers, which was exciting, but I eventually lost control to him, and before I knew it, he had used me to destroy the world as revenge for being experimented on. I managed to separate from him and then travel back in time to prevent all that from happening."

"And now we have to go back to the future and prevent it from happening again," I said.

"Tell me there's another way," Mary said softly.

Richard shook his head.

Mary's face was strained, but she said nothing.

"Way to go, Donnie," Penny scoffed.

Donnie came out of his fog. "I'm not staying, am I?"

"No," Richard said as he put his hand on his son's shoulder. "This is bigger than us now."

Mary returned to the table. "When you first showed signs of having powers, I understood that it meant you didn't belong to me. You belonged to the world. To humanity. You'll *always* be my son, but you have a greater purpose because you are a descendant."

Donnie sniffled but didn't break. "I know."

It was a lot like the conversation I had with my parents right before I left for the academy for sixth grade.

After that, we finished our dinner and got ready to go back to the future.

About an hour later, I was outside behind the cabin. Penny and Noah were still visiting with the Keplers inside, but I just needed some me-time, y'know? Seeing Donnie having to deal with leaving his parents was a little much. . . . It got me missing my own.

There was an open spot in the trees where I could see the North Star clearly. FYI—my dad and I have this thing—we'd both look at the North Star when we missed each other. Knowing we both looked at the same star in the sky helped the lonely times feel *less* lonely.

I probably looked at it way more than he did, but in 1963, I knew he wasn't even around to look at it.

The door swung open behind me, and Headmaster Kepler stepped out. He was alone with a big ol' Sherlock Holmes pipe that he never lit hanging from his mouth. He just chewed on the end of it. Then he dug something out of his pocket and held it out for me.

It was a peanut butter cup.

"Your friends told me these were your favorite," he said, stone-faced. "And Mother likes to keep treats around."

I think he was trying to be nice.

I wasn't sure what to say. In a little bit, we were gonna head back to our time, and I was never gonna see him again.

The stars twinkled overhead as I stared past them into the blackness of space. The old man was still out there somewhere, all by himself behind the universe.

That was how the guy next to me was gonna end up—trapped on the edge of outer space because of a split-second decision to save my life.

Would he take it back if he could?

I wasn't even sure if I deserved it.

I'm just a nobody—a worthless, pathetic nobody.

And he was a superhero who could travel through time.

I couldn't take it anymore.

I *had* to tell him about his future, right?

It was the right thing to do.

Either that, or my guilt finally got the best of me.

I turned to the headmaster and blurted out, *"You're gonna die saving my life!"*

Kepler stopped chewing his pipe. "Mmm, what?"

My hands were shaking. My knees felt weak. I was losing it. "There's a huge explosion in the future, and you take me outside the universe before it kills *me*, but it's gonna kill *you*. Kind of. You're gonna be stuck Outside forever because of it."

I'm not sure why, but I threw my arms around him

and started bawling my eyes out. *"I'm sorry! I'm so, so sorry!"*

I waited for the headmaster to push me off, but . . . that's not what happened.

Instead, he took a knee and looked me in the eye. Then he spoke calmly. "Whatever is going to happen to me *isn't* your fault."

"But it is!" I said like a blubbering idiot. "It's because of me that the explosion even happened!"

Kepler shook his head. "My path is mine to walk alone. And if it leads to my giving my life to save a student, then I will willingly walk that path *every* time."

"I never got the chance to thank you," I said, sniffling.

He smiled.

"You just did," he said.

I hugged the headmaster again. That time he hugged me back. He knew what was gonna happen to him, but that wasn't gonna change what he did.

He was a real hero.

CHAPTER THIRTEEN

It was almost midnight.

Noah, Penny, and I were in front of the cabin, waiting for Donnie to come out. I think he was saying good-bye to his parents. It had to be hard—to know you're leaving your mom and dad like that forever?

Oof.

We were going back to the future, but not *all* the way back—we'd get there during the memorial service right *before* the other Donnie showed up with the Elvis mask. It was the only place we knew the Reaper would be.

"But what about the attack by the Abandoned Children?" Penny asked.

"That's more than eight hours away from when we're showing up," Noah said. "We'll get the Reaper and get out of there before that happens."

"Okay, but can we at least *warn* the school that they're coming?" Penny suggested.

"If we do that, then we risk changing the future," I said. "And that means we might *not* escape with Donnie.

We have to wait until *after* our past selves escape, then we can do whatever we want."

Just then, Donnie rushed out the front door and down the steps with a beekeeper's net in his hands.

"Um, what's with the net?" Penny asked.

"We're gonna snag the Reaper with it," Donnie said.

"Seriously?" I said, taking the net. "We're going up against an alien that destroyed the world, and all you got was a net?"

"It's all we'll need! You heard the old man—the Reaper is a pathetic squid without a host. This'll keep us at a safe distance."

"What about your dad's Power Dampener crossbow thing?" Noah asked. "That'd be *way* more helpful."

"Yeah, right," Donnie said. "I can't sneak that thing outta his hands."

Penny was confused. "Sneak it out? Why not just ask him?"

Donnie stared at the ground but didn't say anything.

Noah and Penny waited for his reason, but I already knew what it was. "Because you're not telling them when we're leaving," I said.

Donnie nodded. "It's easier this way. I know I *have* to go, but if I see my mom cry and say good-bye . . ."

He got too choked up to finish his sentence.

"Okay," was all Noah said.

The four of us walked out to the middle of the yard and stood in a circle, holding hands.

We had our mission.

We knew what we had to do.

Donnie sniffled. "Let's go save the world."

And, in the blink of an eye, the four of us went outside the universe.

CHAPTER FOURTEEN

We walked back to the future as galaxies silently floated in the water beneath our feet.

"How close to the stage can you get us?" I asked.

"I can drop us *under* the stage," Donnie said.

"Is there any chance that you'd drop us *into* the stage?" Noah asked, worried. "Because I don't want to die like that."

Donnie didn't answer as he searched the water. He wasn't much of a talker, but to be fair, his life was a hot mess at that moment.

He was technically an orphan. Headmaster Archer would probably let him live at the academy—maybe he'd even adopt him—but Donnie was still a kid without parents.

"Sorry about your mom and dad," I said.

"Yeah," Donnie said.

"I mean, if it helps, the history books say they disappeared in 1963, too," I said like some dude who always says the *wrong* thing.

Donnie looked back at me. "What?"

Of course, my mouth kept going without my permission. "I don't know, the school's history books say they disappeared a little bit after you did," I said.

Noah and Penny looked at me, like, "*SHUT YOUR MOUTH.*"

"Anywaaay," I sighed, desperately wanting to change

the subject. "Hey, how come you didn't freak out when you fell on the stage? I mean, the *Reaper* was on your *head*."

Donnie continued walking. "I didn't know the Reaper was a thing until an hour ago."

"I can't believe they'd keep that kind of secret from you," Penny said.

"I'm sure there are bigger secrets than that," Donnie said.

BIGGER SECRETS THAN THE REAPER?

NO THANK YOU

I hated *that* idea.

Donnie stopped walking. "We're here," he said, pointing at the reflection in the water. It was the memorial service for Headmaster Kepler. "You guys ready?"

Penny and Noah stood on both sides of Donnie, but

I kept walking. The reflections showed us the past, but they also showed us the future. It was like walking on top of a fortune-teller's crystal ball, and if I went far enough ahead, I could see what was going to happen *after* we caught the Reaper.

I wanted to know if we won.

Or worse, if we lost.

In the water, I saw myself, Donnie, and Dexter getting zapped by Duncan. Me asleep in the nurse's office. The Abandoned Children's attack on the school. Our escape from the lab.

But right after that, the reflections went wonky, flickering random images like a broken TV set. I couldn't make sense of any of it.

My friends caught up to me.

Donnie thought for a moment. "Headmaster Kepler lived his whole life keeping this timeline in check, but . . . he's gone now. The timeline isn't protected."

The images in the water kept changing, morphing into different scenes, sometimes better, sometimes worse. A beautiful, futuristic city with flying cars melted into a city on fire with screaming people. Superheroes and supervillains battling in the clouds like warrior angels. Times Square getting swallowed up by a gigantic black hole.

And then I saw me and my friends. We looked like the Avengers, wearing cool suits and saving the world. But then the image changed again, turning us from the good guys into the bad guys destroying the world.

"What's it mean?" Penny said.

"These are different possible versions of the future," Donnie said. "*Anything* can happen now."

"That's just another way of saying we have no idea what's gonna happen, isn't it?" Penny asked.

The four of us walked back to the reflection of the memorial service. We all took a deep breath and nodded when we were ready.

Donnie tightened his lips and then sank us into the water.

CHAPTER FIFTEEN

We landed in the open grass with a soft thud, the sun shining brightly over our heads. We should've been under the stage, covered in shade, but we weren't.

Donnie messed up.

I knew we were at the funeral because I could hear the same boring story about the old headmaster buzzing through the speaker system. I just didn't know *where* we were at the funeral.

I got on my knees to take in our surroundings. Hopefully, we weren't anywhere close to our past selves.

But, of course, we were *right* behind the last row where they were currently sitting.

"Wait, we're—" I said, but Penny put her hand over my mouth.

"*They can't know we're here,*" she mouthed.

She was right. When we were sitting there earlier, we didn't turn around and see ourselves, so if they did, it would lead to all kinds of problems, jacking up the timeline.

Suddenly, my past self shifted in his seat and started looking over his shoulder. The four of us immediately scooted against the back of the last row, hoping he wouldn't see us.

He didn't.

He's an idiot like that.

Wait, I mean . . . never mind.

Just then, there was a loud crash on the stage, and everything happened exactly the way it did the first time.

Our past selves jumped up from their seats and ran down the aisle as someone up front shouted, "*Get it off me! Get it off!*"

I tried to run after them, but Noah pulled me back. "Not yet, dude! If we go now, everybody will see two versions of us!"

I yanked my arm back. "But if we *don't* go now, we'll lose the Reaper!"

"It's too risky!" Noah said. "Just wait, like, thirty seconds!"

Didn't he realize that every second counted? That waiting was a *bigger* risk? He'd understand after I had the Reaper in custody.

I acted cool, like I was gonna duck down again, but then I grabbed the beekeeper's net from Donnie and took off down a different aisle.

The past versions of ourselves were already at the stage, and I even heard myself say, "Holy donks," from the speakers.

I slid to a stop behind the first row so they wouldn't

see me. Another second passed, and then they all made their way to the buffet tables.

I was clear.

And it was go-time.

I crawled around, searching for any signs of a slithering squid, but there was nothing.

The Reaper was invisible when he got me Outside, and he was invisible when he came back with Donnie. I was trying to find a patch of grass that moved unnaturally.

"Where is he?" Noah said when he finally arrived. "Do you see anything?"

"Nothing yet," I said.

"You *probably* scared him off by going all gung ho," Noah said, annoyed.

"We *probably* lost him because you *didn't*," I said, even *more* annoyed.

Noah pushed his fingers through the grass. "You're gonna get us all killed with that attitude."

What was his deal?

We were running out of time, and all he wanted to do was lecture me?

If we didn't find the Reaper now, then he'd be gone forever. Or at least until he decided to destroy the planet again.

I watched the ground carefully for movement. The wind blew gently, making the grass blades sway softly.

I figured one of two things—one, if the Reaper was

crawling around, then we'd see grass bend as he pushed it aside. Or two, if the Reaper was keeping perfectly still, then only the grass underneath him would be frozen, like a dead spot.

But then I realized a third option—squids don't become invisible. They use camouflage to blend in with their surroundings. They make themselves *look like* the things around them. I learned that on a little something called "the Internet."

I was super into squids for a while, don't ask why.

If that was the case, then the Reaper's body would look like gently blowing grass. The only way to see him would be to lay my head on the ground and look for a small hump of earth that was out of place.

My only hope was that the Reaper's alien squid body acted like an *Earth* squid's body.

And that's when I saw it. A smooth lump that wasn't moving, except it *looked* like it was. On the surface were patches of green and brown colors, quivering like the grass around it.

I slowly raised the beekeeper's net as Noah, Penny, and Donnie watched with wide eyes—they knew it was about to get real.

Then I screamed, slamming the pathetic net down over the lump.

The Reaper's skin flashed red, and his eyes opened like two huge bulges on his head. He tore right through the net and shot through the grass like Sonic the freakin' Hedgehog.

Donnie dove after it but missed. Noah shot fire bullets from his fingertips, but none of them hit the Reaper.

"Your aim needs work!" Penny said, leaping for the alien just before it reached the edge of the forest, landing right on top of it. Noah and Donnie jumped in just as I got there.

The three of them wrestled the Reaper, but it was eight tentacles against three kids, and the tentacles were winning.

That's when the four of us realized the same thing at the exact same time—that the Reaper *wasn't* a weak little squid—he was *extremely* strong.

Headmaster Kepler was wrong.

Very, very wrong!

The Reaper slipped his tentacles around my friends, pulling each kid off his body one at a time. Noah was the last to get tossed, and then the alien went for the forest again.

Without thinking, I dropped onto the squid, pinning him under my legs. He squirmed a bit but stopped when we made eye contact.

That's when the weirdest thing happened.

A little slit opened under his eyes, and he smiled.

I sprang back, but the alien was attached to me, wrapping its creepy tentacles around my arms.

"No, no, no, no!" I screamed. *"Help me!"*

Noah, Penny, and Donnie grabbed his body and pulled in the opposite direction until every last suction cup popped off my skin.

The Reaper shook himself free and came at me again, but I was gone, sprinting through the forest like crazy to get away.

It didn't matter how fast I was. The Reaper was faster. He dashed in front of me and behind me, jumping from tree to tree, using his tentacles to swing and slingshot himself all over the place, like a cartoon character hopped up on too much caffeine.

He was playing with me.

Suddenly, Noah grabbed me from behind and lifted me up, leaving a stream of fire behind us as we flew toward the sky.

The Reaper swung higher to keep up with us. When we were past the top of the forest, I thought we were clear until I looked at my foot.

He was on my ankle!

AND HE WAS STILL SMILING.

I kicked my foot, but it didn't do much.

The creature climbed my leg as I wriggled in Noah's grip. I tried to pry him off, but there was no way I could compete with eight different tentacles snaking around different parts of my body.

I freaked out, twisting and turning and trying my best to keep the alien from making it to my head.

"Ben, stop!" Noah said. "I can't hold you when—"

Noah's grasp slipped, and I dropped.

The Reaper enveloped his tentacles around me like I was a mummy. Then he slid himself over my face just like he did when we were Outside. I was powerless to stop him.

My body was suddenly yanked upward like it was attached to a yo-yo and everything became a blur of white and blue colors that quickly faded to black.

I clenched my eyes shut, hoping that whatever was

gonna happen would happen fast. And I hate to say it, but now that the Reaper was on my head, a quick and painless death would've been the best-case scenario.

The last thing I heard was the sound of his voice, not from my ears, but from the inside of my skull.

CHAPTER SIXTEEN

When my body came to a sudden stop, I finally opened my eyes. Crazy that the whole thing lasted ten, maybe fifteen seconds, but somehow it was nighttime, and there were stars in the sky.

Even crazier was that I wasn't in any pain.

There were no signs of my friends anywhere.

And as for the Reaper . . . there wasn't any sign of him either.

I pushed myself up, feeling light-headed.

Literally.

My head *felt* lighter.

Actually, *everything* felt lighter.

A barren gray desert surrounded me on all sides, and my arms floated like I was underwater even though I wasn't.

No forest. No plants. No colors.

No *nothing*.

I was definitely NOT in Colorado anymore.

I tried jumping to my feet, but I drifted off the

ground like I was weightless. Then I tried running, but my body barely moved, like I was stuck in some kind of slow-motion nightmare.

None of it made any sense.

That is, until I looked up.

. . . And saw planet Earth floating silently in the night sky.

And if Earth was up there, it could only mean . . .

I panicked.

It couldn't have been real.

It had to be a dream.

I wasn't even wearing a space suit!

How was I on the moon *without* a space suit?

I was in pure freak-out mode when things got even worse. I heard that voice in my head again. The one I had heard when I was falling through the trees not even a minute ago. The voice of the Reaper.

"HELLO, BEN," he said.

The fact that I could hear his voice inside my skull meant *he was still on my head.*

"STAY CALM," he said with a low, creepy voice. **"EVERY-THING WILL BE OKAY."**

"Get off!" I said, feeling his body right on my face.

He was squishy and completely draped over my dome. I slid my fingers up my cheeks, under the Reaper's gross squid body, and started pulling him off my skin.

"No, no, no, don't!" he shouted in my head. But his voice wasn't so scary that time. It was bright and earnest, kind of like it came from a kid.

I stopped for a second, surprised at his change in tone, but then it went back to being all goth.

"Uh, I mean, stop that at once, thick-skulled human!" the Reaper commanded.

But I didn't listen.

The Reaper's tentacles wrapped around my wrists and yanked my arms back. *"You're acting like a baby!"* the Reaper shrieked, dropping the Darth Vader voice completely.

"Takes one to know one!" I said. I knew I needed a new tactic, so I tried face-planting into the ground, but the low gravity made that idea worthless.

Then he used my own hands to punch me in the face over and over again.

We both screamed as I shook my head back and forth. When I stopped, the moon was spinning, and the Reaper was groaning. I looked at Earth.

Every single person I knew and cared for was on that little blue marble. And there I was on the surface of the moon with the chance to save ALL their lives.

It just meant that I'd have to give up mine.

And I was okay with that.

I grabbed his squishy body again. "Get your butt off my face!" I said, squeezing hard.

"*Stop!*" the Reaper said, laughing. *"That's my ink sac!"*

Black fluid shot out from under him and splattered down my cheeks. Little blobs of dark liquid floated in front of us.

The Reaper howled with laughter as I sat in shock. It was so gross, but I wasn't exactly sure *how* gross, y'know what I mean?

What *is* squid ink?

Is it pee?

Like . . . did the bad guy just pee all over me?

I was probably better off not knowing.

The Reaper caught his breath. *"Are you finished?"*

I tried to be brave. "You might as well kill me now, because there's no way you're using me to destroy the world!"

"I'm NOT going to kill you," the Reaper said. *"I used you to fly us out here, but I can't control you if you're dead. Dead bodies don't work the same, don't ask how I know. So if you die out here, I'm sort of stuck."*

"So I'm your ride back?? Why'd you bring us out here at all, then?? Why wouldn't you take us somewhere else on Earth??"

"Well, maybe I wasn't thinking clearly since that fire kid was trying to kill ME!"

"Noah wasn't trying to kill you! He was trying to catch you!"

Dang it!

I said too much, and now the Reaper knew Noah's name. I stopped talking, but did that matter? Could that thing on my head read my mind?

"Just so you know, I can't read your mind. Our bond doesn't work like that," the Reaper said.

"Then how'd you know I was thinking it?"

"It kind of FELT like you were?"

Fine.

He couldn't read my mind.

I could use that to my advantage.

I sat on the ground, folded my arms, and pouted like a baby. Let's see if the Reaper likes the *silent treatment.*

"Good! Don't talk!" he said, annoyed. *"All you need to do is listen. I'm not going to hurt you. You'd already*

be dead if I wanted to kill you. It PAINS me to say this, but I need your HELP."

"Yeah right," I said. "You need my help with destroying the world."

Obviously, I'm not very good at giving the silent treatment.

"I know you don't want to hurt anybody," the Reaper said. "I know you won't hurt ME."

"What's that mean?" I asked.

"You're not like the ones who captured me. The ones who locked me in a cage to study me. Kept me from returning to my home. My friends. My family. They chopped my tentacles off over and over to study my DNA."

"But they grew back!" I said like that was a good reason.

"Which is how they did it hundreds of times," the Reaper said. "But you're not like them. You won't do that."

"No," I said quietly. "That's . . . pretty uncool."

"I know YOU just want to get rid of me, Ben. Which is why I can trust you because you only want me to GO AWAY."

I hated that I had nowhere to run. Nowhere to hide. I was forced to have this conversation with the Reaper.

"You're not wrong," I said. "But what do you want?"

The alien squid paused. "I just want to go home."

"I see what's going on here," I said. "You dragged me out to the moon, and now you need me to get you back, but then you're gonna use me to murder billions of people!"

"WHAT are you talking about?"

"You're gonna give me powers and then use me to destroy the world! You already did that with Headmaster Kepler, but I'm not gonna fall for it!"

"What do you mean I already did that?"

"When you *invaded* Earth! Headmaster Kepler told us all about it!"

"What, the guy with the eyebrows? I wasn't INVADING! I was EXPLORING!"

"No! You used Donald Kepler to destroy the world! He told us everything! That's why he went back in time and caught you *before* you could . . . do . . . the thing . . . and so you . . ."

Okay, wait . . .

Headmaster Kepler went back in time and caught the Reaper *before* any of that happened. So technically the Reaper never did *anything* wrong.

At least not *yet.*

"But don't you want revenge for what they did to you?" I asked. "I mean, your name is the Reaper because you murdered the world."

"My name is NIX, you jerk," he said. *"And all I wanna do . . . is find my ship and go home."*

I didn't know what to think, because it didn't sound like he was lying, but most good liars don't.

"How do I know I can trust you?" I asked.

"You don't, I guess," Nix answered honestly. *"But I never did anything wrong. The only thing I'm guilty of is being curious about your planet. And for that, they chopped me apart repeatedly and then abandoned me in that dark place."*

He was talking about the Outside.

There I went, feeling sorry for the bad guy again, just like I did with Abigail. With Angel. And with Coach Lindsay.

I had no idea what to do.

I know what Headmaster Kepler would've done—he would've torn the alien off his head and let them both die in outer space.

But I wasn't Kepler.

I was me.

And if there was *any* chance the squid wasn't the villain everybody thought he was . . .

Wasn't that a chance worth taking?

"I want to make you a deal," Nix said bluntly.

I took a deep breath, hoping I wouldn't regret my decision. If I was wrong, then humanity was doomed. But if I was right . . .

I mean, I fully understood the weight of my decision, but I had to go with my gut on this.

"I'm listening. . . ." I said.

"I'll give you powers for the day. Free rein. But in return, you help me find my ship so I can go back to my planet."

Powers for the day *would* be awesome, and there was still the Abandoned Children to worry about . . .

"And what if I say no?" I asked.

"*I mean, it'll be easier if you work with me,*" Nix said.

I wasn't sure if that was a threat or not.

I sighed. "What time is it? How long have we been on the moon?"

"*Only a few minutes,*" Nix said.

Donnie took us back to the funeral around noon. The Abandoned Children were going to attack at eight p.m., and I had no idea where they were at the moment, so that gave me about eight hours until they hit the school.

That's eight hours for me to learn how to be a kick-butt superhero.

Nix's deal suddenly sounded a little sweeter.

Obviously, I wasn't sure if he could be trusted.

But I guess I was about to find out.

CHAPTER SEVENTEEN

Noon.

Eight hours until the attack.

I zoomed through space like a rocket, going so fast that I could actually see planet Earth growing larger. Every molecule in my body screamed for joy as I held my arms over my head, flying like Superman.

My bond with Nix gave me superpowers. I could fly,

I had superstrength, and I could control his tentacles with practice. As a bonus, he kept himself camouflaged on my head so nobody could see him. He was basically invisible.

And so, after two long years of watching kids at Kepler Academy level-up their powers—of getting left behind, of being a nobody—I was finally getting my shot.

I wasn't just another kid anymore.

I *finally* had superpowers.

Nailed it.

As I entered Earth's atmosphere, I spun, twirling a trail of fire behind me. I didn't care if anybody saw—actually, I *wanted* them to see—because if a tree falls in the forest and nobody's around to hear it, does it make a sound?

I thought about finding Penny and Noah first, but then it would turn into this whole big thing where I had to explain what was going on with Nix. And I don't know, I just figured I'd wait until *after* I saved the school from the Abandoned Children to say anything to them.

Plus, I wanted to practice my powers on my own without anyone telling me what to do, which seemed to be Noah's new life goal.

I flew over mountains, followed rivers, and dipped into valleys until I was over the ocean. I don't know which one. I actually had no idea where in the world I was, but I didn't even care.

I went above the clouds, looking for a city where I could be a superhero. It didn't take long.

"*You should probably slow down,*" Nix said as I flew toward the city.

"Roger, roger," I said, trying to ease up a little.

"*No, FOR REAL, slow down!*" he shouted.

It was harder than I thought.

Like, *way* harder.

So hard that I actually lost control and started tumbling through the air like a rag doll.

"*No, no, no, no, no!*" Nix said.

I could feel him try to slow us down, but it was too late. We hit the ground like a cannonball, kicking up an explosion of dirt right in the middle of a park full of screaming people.

I lay there for a second, feeling *almost* no pain at all.

I should've been squashed like a bug, but I wasn't!

"You're gonna have to work on those landings," Nix said.

"I'll get it," I said, shooting back into the sky.

I needed action! Excitement! Someone to save! And as if the universe could read my mind, I found exactly what I was looking for as I flew over the downtown area—a robbery at the First Bank of Portland!

How cool was that? A *bank* robbery!

I mean, that *wasn't* cool at all.

But it was cool for me.

Not that I *wanted* bad things to happen.

Because I didn't.

Except I *kiiind* of did, but only that *one time.*

Um, anyway, I landed on the roof of the bank, its alarms blaring, just as the robbers scrambled toward their getaway car.

They were typical comic book baddies—big dudes in ski masks, waving guns around, and carrying bags of cash. Their car's tires screeched as it took off.

"What do I do?" I asked.

"Well, you can do it the easy way," Nix said. *"Or the hard way."*

"Let's start with the easy way."

"Now we're talkin'. Let's go kill them and get the heck outta here."

"What!? No! I'm not killing anybody!"

"But . . ." Nix paused. *"That's the EASY way."*

"Nope. Gotta go with the hard way, then."

"Okay, well, that means I'm all out of ideas."

I jumped off the building and zipped past the get-away car, landing in the road in front of the robbers, and then I put my hands up to stop their car.

I meant to do it gently, but I kind of miscalculated how fast they were going. Their car buckled when it hit me. The whole front end wrapped around my body as bits of broken windshield shot past my face.

AWESOME.

CRASH!

In the blink of an eye, it was over.

And I was fine.

Their car was so bent up that I had to pry the engine apart just so I could move. As the dust settled, I made my way around to the driver's door.

I was about to rip it off and say something heroic until I saw the guys inside. They were groaning in pain. None of them reached for their weapons or tried to escape. They were just sitting there, horribly, horribly injured.

I kinda felt bad about it.

"Nice!" Nix said. *"You took 'em out without even touching them! I might be a fan of the hard way now."*

As I reached for the driver's door, somebody grabbed the back of my pants, hoisted me into the air, and said, "I believe the local police department has a room with *your* name on it, criminal scum."

It was a *big* man.

Big muscles. Big jaw. Big voice.

Big *everything.*

He had a mask over his face and a skintight black

costume with a giant *M* on the chest along with a bright yellow utility belt around his waist.

I couldn't believe my eyes.

I was staring at a real-life superhero.

And he thought *I* was the bad guy.

CHAPTER EIGHTEEN

The man's voice boomed like Adam West's Batman.

From the way he was carrying me with one hand, I knew his power was superstrength. He *had* to have been a descendant.

"*This guy is nothing compared to us. Beat him down, and let's roll,*" Nix joked.

At least I *think* it was a joke.

"*I'm* not the bad guy!" I said.

The man cocked his head. "You *aren't* aiding or abetting these criminals?"

"No! I was trying to stop them!" I said, freeing myself from his grip. I flexed my power by floating in the air in front of him.

I heard a loud groan from inside the robbers' car, which made my stomach churn. I might've seriously hurt them.

The masked man laughed heartily as he patted his belly. "Well, good on you, chum! I can see by your power that you're clearly a descendant of the Seven Keys, and you've chosen the side of good over evil!"

I stared at him for a second.

The man cocked an eye. "You think? You're still un-decided about which side you've chosen?"

"No, that's not—" I said. I was gonna have to be a little more sneaky when I talked to Nix. "Never mind."

Standing in front of me was a legit superhero with real powers, which Kepler Academy strictly forbade (is that a word?). . . . So how'd *this dude* get a free pass?

Sirens blared as police cars turned the corner.

The man gasped and took off down an alley.

He dove headfirst into a Dumpster. Then he peeked over the top and waved for me to follow.

Ah, okay.

He didn't get a free pass.

He was just doing it on his own.

I looked at the bad guys in the car. I didn't hurt them on purpose, but I also didn't want to go to jail, so I ran into the alley and hid *behind* the Dumpster rather than *inside* it because I care about things like good hygiene.

Cop cars and an ambulance pulled up, and within minutes, the robbers were hauled away to a hospital.

Once the action died down, the masked man stood up, covered head to toe in Dumpster juices. Banana peels and crumpled tissues stuck to his body. "Mmmm. Lady Justice has smiled upon us today, my new little friend."

As weird as he was, I was pumped about meeting this guy. He was a real-life superhero living my dream—costume, mask, chest logo—the whole shebang!

I *knew* superheroes existed!

And I just happened to run into one *right* after getting a power of my own?

Come on.

That's not a coincidence.

That's *fate*.

I held out my hand. "My name is Ben Braver, sir!"

"*Don't say anything about me,*" Nix said.

"Obvi," I said to Nix.

"Names aren't as obvious as you think," the man said as he shook my hand. "Pleased to meet you, Ben Braver! You can call me *MAGNIFIC*."

How cool was that name?

Magnific sprang from the Dumpster and took a bite of a half-eaten banana he'd peeled off his body, murmuring as he chewed. "Yum . . . this is *delectable*. Want some?"

"Uh, thanks," I said, taking the banana and ignoring Nix, who was making barf noises in my head. When Magnific wasn't looking, I tossed the half-eaten fruit back into the Dumpster.

I couldn't have met a real superhero at a better time, especially because I was still a noob with my powers. He could teach me so much of what the academy never did.

Magnific put his hands on his hips and posed majestically. "It's been a pleasure, Ben Braver. And I wish you luck on your journey."

"Wait!" I said. "Let me hang out with you! Just for the day! Like, let me be your sidekick!"

Magnific scratched his chin as he studied me.

"Come on!" Nix shouted in my head. *"Let's ditch this guy! He's only gonna hold you back!"*

I spun around so Magnific wouldn't hear me. "No!" I whispered. "I'm staying here! You have no idea how *huge* this is for me!"

"Do you have any idea how huge it is for you that I'M here?" Nix said, annoyed.

He had a point.

We both had points.

But my point was more important than his point.

"Being a do-gooder *does* get lonely, and no super-hero should be a lone wolf!" Magnific said. "I'll take you under my wing, little bird, but only if you're not skipping school! As George Washington Carver once said, education is the key to unlocking the golden door of freedom!"

Yeah. He was pretty cheesy.

"What time is it?" I asked.

Magnific looked at the sky instead of a clock. "A little past noon," he said like some kind of master Boy Scout.

The Abandoned Children weren't going to attack the academy until eight p.m., which gave me a little less than eight hours to learn from Magnific and master my new powers. That was plenty of time and a *very* mature thing for me to do in the meantime.

Noah would probably lecture me about it, because that's all he does anymore, but I'm pretty sure he'd get over it after he saw my new powers.

"I'm good," I said.

"Then come along, small child!" Magnific said. "We have much work to do and less time to do it in."

CHAPTER NINETEEN

Magnific and I sat on a bench along the street, watching people give us strange looks as they passed. He was nibbling on a second Dumpster banana, trying to make it last as long as possible.

"*Welp, this sucks,*" Nix said in my brain. "*I give you the power to enslave the entire human race, and you're just gonna sit here?*"

I hoped he was being sarcastic.

"Yup," I said.

"Should I just go find someone else?" Nix asked.

I stood up from the bench and smiled at Magnific. "Excuse me a second."

I walked just out of earshot of the real-life super-hero, then I quietly went off on Nix.

"Look, man," I huffed. "You said you didn't want to hurt anybody, but now it sounds like you're super into it with all this talk about enslaving the human race!"

"I'm just saying! Aren't there better things to do?"

"Not for me, no! And what do you care if I choose to sit here with Magnific as long as I help you find your ship afterward?"

"I don't! As long as you help me later, you can nap all day for all I care!"

"Good!"

"Good!"

I returned to Magnific with a smile still on my face. "Sorry about that. . . . I, uh, had to fart."

Why would I say that??

Luckily, Magnific didn't hear it. He was too busy ad-miring the fruit in his hand. "I *like* bananas. They're perfectly suited to fit the human hand. I also like lem-ons and pineapples—oh! Perhaps I just love the color yellow! *Cheese* is yellow, and I *like* cheese!"

"Yeah, no, it's great," I said.

Magnific turned to me. "You sound down in the

dumps, little guy. You want adventure, don't you? It'll happen soon enough! Being a superhero is about patience."

"Can't we just *make* the adventure?" I asked.

"*Yes*," Nix said in my head. "*We can.*"

"That's not how it works, my eager companion," Magnific said. "The adventure will find *you*."

"Just like with the bank robbery," I said.

Magnific leaned back. "Ah, yes, that *was* an adventure and a *rare* one, at that."

I guess I knew bank robberies didn't happen every day, but I couldn't help but hope that maybe there was another one on the other side of town. And yes, I know how bad it sounded that I *wanted* someone to rob a bank, but only so I could *stop* them!

"Maybe there's a store getting burgled," I said. "Or a *mugging*! Ohhh, a *mugging* would be *perfect*!"

Magnific looked at me like I was crazy. "Those kinds of crimes don't happen as often as you'd think, friend. You know how many bank robberies I've foiled in my twenty years of doing this?"

"How many?"

"Just one," he said. "And that was thirty minutes ago."

It took twenty years until Magnific came across a bank robbery. . . . But it had taken me only a few minutes. Hopefully, my luck was just better than his. Or wait, would that make it worse? Whatever. You get it.

He suddenly sat up, snapping his head to the left like a dog that just saw a squirrel.

"What is it?" I said.

He held his finger up to hush me and then narrowed his eyes, listening intently to something I couldn't hear. After a moment, he nodded. Then he jumped up from the bench. "Quickly, Ben Braver, before it's too late."

"Okay, but stop using my full name!" I said.

Finally!

We were on our way to bust some criminals!

Magnific tore down the sidewalk.

I stayed close behind him, running instead of flying because I didn't want to tip off the bad guys that some superheroes were coming to knock their heads around.

At the stoplight, Magnific put his arm out and kept me from charging into the street. He jogged in place, staring at the stoplight.

"What're you waiting for?" I said.

"The crosswalk to change," he said.

"Wait, are you serious?"

The sign switched from STOP to GO, and Magnific dashed off again. I did my best to keep up, but he was fast.

Like, crazy fast.

And I was starting to lose him.

He was half a block ahead of me when Nix said, *"Why aren't you flying? This would be a lot easier if you flew."*

"I'm *his* sidekick!" I said. "So I need to follow *his* lead!"

"You lack ambition!" Nix said as he used his invisible tentacles to slingshot me across the block.

I landed perfectly next to Magnific, where he was stopped in front of some skaters chillin' at a shopping mall.

"Don't use my real name!" I said.

"Yes, of course, you'll want to protect your identity!" he said with a wink. He looked at the group of skaters. "What I meant to say was, excellent timing, *Beanie Weenie!*"

Great.

A sidekick's hero name is just as important as the

principles they stand for. . . . And I had just been dubbed BEANIE WEENIE. At least the *B* matched my shirt.

I looked around, trying to find the criminals Magnific was about to nab, but all I saw were the skaters on the sidewalk.

I couldn't believe it. I was out of breath and nursing a side cramp because some kids were skateboarding in a parking lot?

Magnific sneered at the teenagers but didn't say anything. He snatched a board from the leader of the gang, who didn't fight back.

Nobody said a thing. The skaters. Magnific. Me. We watched quietly to see what Magnific was gonna do with the board.

Nix squirmed as he spoke in my brain. *"Okay, let's do this. Take out the leader—don't KILL him—just horribly injure. See? I'm learning."*

"I'm not doing that," I whispered.

"Of course you won't, Beanie Weenie," Nix said. *"Because you don't do ANYTHING I tell you."*

That squid was getting on my nerves.

At last, Magnific spoke. "This is a nice board," he said. "Be a shame if something . . . *bad* happened to it."

The skater eyeballed Magnific. "Bad things happen to good boards all the time, brah. That's life."

The two of them stared each other down. I wasn't sure what was going on, but it was definitely weird.

Then, out of nowhere, Magnific threw the skateboard under his feet and proceeded to absolutely *kill it* with his skills.

Seriously.

The jacked beast in the tights could shred.

The teenagers chanted his name as he kicked some flips and popped some shove-its. It was pretty obvious that they all knew one another. Magnific wasn't there to bust them—he was there to dazzle them.

When he was done, he kicked the board up and

caught it with his hand. Then he gave it to the leader of the skaters.

"Sick moves, homie," the skater said.

"Can't knock the hustle," Magnific said with a smirk. "Now get movin' before mall security comes."

The teenagers laughed but didn't argue. They all hopped onto their boards and skated off, leaving behind some plastic water bottles.

"Another job well done," Magnific said, dusting his hands off.

"Wait, what just happened?" I said. "I thought you were running to stop a crime!"

"I never said that," Magnific said.

"What was the point of this?"

"Being a good role model was the point," Magnific said like it should've been obvious.

He pulled a wrinkly grocery bag out of his utility belt, which BTW, now that I got a closer look, was just a fancy-looking fanny pack. Then he collected the bottles the skaters left behind.

"That, and they were loitering," Magnific added.

"Great," I said. "The mall parking lot is safe for all shoppers now."

Magnific pulled the lid off a nearby trash can, but instead of putting his sack of bottles in it, he started taking bottles out, adding them to his collection.

I watched as he did this to every garbage can he passed as we made our way down the sidewalk.

At one point, he started humming different Disney songs to himself. He was obviously having a delightful time, but I, on the other hand, was beginning to wonder if Nix might've been right. . . .

Maybe trailing this dude wasn't the best idea I'd ever had.

CHAPTER TWENTY

3 p.m.

Five hours until the attack.

We spent the next two and a half hours performing random acts of kindness—the kind of random acts that *didn't* require powers to perform.

I'm pretty sure Nix even fell asleep on my head for a bit. I heard him snoring in my brain, but maybe he was just being sarcastic.

We helped some people cross a street, changed a flat tire, complimented a street performer, listened to an old

guy tell war stories while playing chess, fed some ducks, gave directions to a lost family, held a door open for somebody in a wheelchair, finished mowing some lady's yard, helped a mom with her crying baby, and walked a dude's dog at the park.

Oh, and Magnific also filled two more bags with empty bottles. He never said what he was doing, but it was obvious his mission was to recycle all of it.

It was a pretty full day of *not fighting crime.*

I was starting to get antsy. I didn't have all the time in the world, and I'd already wasted three hours of it. If Magnific wasn't gonna bust some bad-guy bottoms soon, I was gonna have to bail on the dude.

Outside the city library, Magnific stopped. He squinted and snarled like a growling lion. "There's *trouble* brewing in the library. . . ."

Finally!

Uh . . . a *second* finally.

The first didn't count because nothing happened.

But, finally! Something cool was happening! What else can *"There's* trouble *brewing in the library . . ."* mean??

"How do you know?" I asked, peering through the tinted windows.

"I can *feel* it," he said, setting his three grocery bags down by the entrance. He pushed his way through the revolving doors.

I cracked my knuckles and followed his lead.

"*The library's quiet,*" Nix said, all serious. "*Too quiet.*"

People sat at desks, working on homework or business stuff or whatever people go to the library to work on. Others stood in aisles, looking for books or glancing our way.

Nobody batted an eye that a huge dude wearing tights just strolled through the front doors.

"Keep your eyes peeled," Magnific said. "I smell an *ambush. . . .*"

"For real?" I said. "Is it a trap? Do they know you're coming?"

He nodded slowly, scanning the room. "Oh, they know."

"But why would they set a trap for you in the library?" I asked.

And then I got my answer.

A swarm of little kids burst from one of the aisles and ran out to Magnific. They jumped all over him until he pretended to fall over, defeated. They were young, probably prekindergarten. Their moms and dads hung back, watching with smiles.

Magnific reached his arm up. "You've bested me, children! I give up! I give up!"

The librarian smiled as she walked up to us. "Give Magnific some space, guys."

"It's quite all right," he said, standing, doing that hands-on-his-hips pose again. And *that's* when he started *singing. "Who's the man who's ter-ri-fic?"*

All the kids, *plus* the librarian, responded by clapping their hands and singing. *"Mag-ni-fic! Mag-ni-fic!"*

They knew who he was.

It wasn't their first rodeo.

Everyone cheered, *including* Nix.

My mind was blown, but not in a *whoa-I-just-learned-something-cool* kind of way. It was more like a *what-the-heck-am-I-watching-this-is-uncomfortable-I-want-to-go-home-now* kind of way.

Magnific led everyone to the children's book section

of the library. I passed a cardboard poster that had a picture of Magnific holding a book.

Everyone settled in for story time as Magnific introduced himself, then he gave me a slap on the back and told the group I was his sidekick for the day.

The librarian handed Magnific a book that had a bunch of cartoon lions on it. He held it in front of himself and read the title out loud.

"*The Trouble with Lying Lions!*" he said, winking at me. "I told you there was *trouble* brewing here."

I groaned.

But Nix laughed.

For some reason, that little squid was suddenly interested in what was going on. He even got off my dome so he could hide on top of a bookshelf to get closer to Magnific—Nix *wanted* to hear the story! He didn't bother camouflaging himself, but he still stayed in the shadows. He had a smile on his face and everything.

I sat way in the back as Magnific read the dumb lion book out loud. He was super into it, too, using growly voices for different characters, acting out scenes, and jumping all over the place like some kind of clown.

I mean, it was cool, don't get me wrong.

But it just wasn't *superhero* cool, y'know?

Anyone can read a book to a kid.

THERE'S PROBABLY A VALUABLE LESSON HERE, BUT I DON'T WANT TO THINK ABOUT IT.

About thirty minutes later, Magnific wrapped up his library visit with hugs and high fives.

Nix returned to my head. *"Wow, that was great!"*

"For real?" I asked.

"Yeah, for real!"

I walked down one of the aisles so nobody would

hear me talking to the squid. "I didn't think you'd be a fan of story time," I said to him.

"Why? Because I'm an alien? Because I've been stuck Outside for who knows how long and I miss my parents and that reminded me of when my dad used to read books to me before bed?"

Was it possible that he was telling the truth?

What if the guy who became a villain in an alternate timeline *didn't* become a villain in mine?

That might be too much for my tiny brain.

Outside, Magnific grabbed his bags of bottles and continued down the sidewalk with a hop in his step.

"The library poster said you do this every day," I said, following him.

"That's right," he said proudly.

"So then . . . do you have a job?"

"This *is* my job, chum."

I didn't think he was getting my drift. "Okay, but what about when you're *not* Magnific? Your alter ego?"

My question didn't make sense to him. "I never understood the point of having an alter ego. I am who I am, and I *am* Magnific."

"But what's your real name?" I asked, frustrated.

"Magnific!" he said, and then he quietly sang his theme song. *"Who's the man who's ter-ri-fic?"*

Nix sang along in my head. *"Mag-ni-fic! Mag-ni-fic!"*

"Stop singing!" I snipped at both of them. "What about *before* you were Magnific? What was your real name when you went to the academy?"

"Ah," he said. "That wasn't an alter ego. It was a former life that I'm no longer attached to."

"Whoa, wait. Are you saying you're Magnific 24/7?"

"As long as people are in need, Magnific will be there, and people are *always* in need."

I couldn't believe my earballs.

First, the supervillain alien symbiote turned out to be a homesick squid, and now a real-life superhero turns out to be a loony tune in tights. "And you've been doing this for twenty years?" I asked.

"Sure have," he said without missing a beat.

"Then you're loaded, right?" I said. "There's no way you can do this full-time without having *tons* of bread in the bank."

He laughed mightily. "I'm sorry to disappoint, but there's not a penny to my name!"

"But then where do you live? How do you eat?"

"The *streets* are my home," he said. "The city takes care of me, feeds me when I'm hungry. *She* is my mother."

My jaw nearly hit the floor.

I'd been job-shadowing a hobo for the past three hours!

CHAPTER TWENTY-ONE

'm not sure why, but the thought of Magnific's *not* having an alter ego made me sad. Maybe it was that I couldn't imagine myself being 100 percent devoted to being a superhero.

No breaks? No time for buddies? No time for video games, movies, or comics?

That sounded like the *worst*!

"I thought you'd at least be a secret billionaire or something."

"That would be convenient, wouldn't it? With billions of dollars, I could reshape this entire city by giving money to those in need!"

"Uh, no, with billions of dollars, you could afford *cool gadgets* and *tank-cars* to help you beat up bad guys," I said. "Just like Batman."

"I never understood Batman," Magnific said. "With that much money, I'd build schools. Homeless shelters. Parks. He could help more people by donating money instead of buying bat-copters and shark repellent."

Auugh! Now Magnific was ruining Batman for me!

Magnific was more *real* than I was comfortable with. He had his way of doing things, that's for sure, but it wasn't what *I* needed. The Abandoned Children were going to attack in about four hours. I had powers, and I had to practice using them.

"Welllp," I said with a stretch. "It's been fun, but I should probably make like a banana and split."

Magnific laughed. "Bananas *are* delish, but the fun has just begun, my young friend!"

I sighed again.

Loudly.

Because I was *annoyed*.

"You're perturbed," Magnific said sadly.

"I just expected a little more . . ." I paused, thinking

of the right word to use so there wouldn't be any confusion.

"*Combat?*" Nix suggested.

"Combat," I repeated out loud.

"Aha!" Magnific snapped his fingers. "Then you're in luck! If it's combat you seek, then it's combat you shall receive at our next location! Just stick with me a little longer and you'll learn the real importance of being a superhero!"

Okay. There was no way I could misinterpret that.

"Fine," I said. "But if this isn't combat, then I'm out."

Magnific smiled.

We walked a few more blocks, sprinkling some kindness to anyone we could. I got into it, but only because I knew we were on our way to *combat*.

When we turned a corner, I saw a line of people outside a building, waiting to get in. They looked pretty rough, with torn-up clothes, and nobody was smiling.

At least not until they saw Magnific.

Their faces lit up at the sight of him, and just like the kids at the library, they knew him by name.

Some shook his hand. Some bumped his fist. Others high-fived. He even shared a secret handshake with one of them. I smiled politely and said hello to anyone who noticed me.

Finally, Magnific waved and told everybody that he'd see them inside.

"Inside?" I repeated. "You said we were on our way to *combat*."

Magnific held the door open for me. "We are, Ben Braver! We're here to *combat* homelessness."

O. M. G.

That was it.

I was done.

Maybe Magnific's superpower was that he could twist words.

I was about to unleash a tantrum the likes of which the world had *never* seen before, but right at the last second, some woman popped up out of nowhere.

"Magnific!" she said as she danced her way to us. "What's up!"

Magnific shimmied a bit. "Livin' the dream, Lydia!"

"Who's this guy?" Lydia asked, pointing finger-guns at me. "Wait, let me guess! You're the *sidekick*! Mini-Magnific!"

Magnific let out a bold laugh. "Brilliant wordplay!"

I hung my head sheepishly. "Uh, no, my name's Ben Braver."

"He *is* my sidekick today," Magnific said.

"Is that so?" Lydia said, playfully eyeballing me. "You wanna be a superhero, too?"

I don't know why, but I was embarrassed. "Sort of."

"Then you're with the right guy," Lydia said. "There's no better teacher than Magnific. He spends more time volunteering here than all the other volunteers *combined*."

"That's not true," Magnific said.

Lydia smiled. "Don't listen to him," she said to me. "He's here *every day* at four forty-five on the dot! Like he's a walking clock!"

Magnific shrugged.

Lydia took me behind a long table with trays of food on it. Then she told me what to do—not that I was looking for a job.

"Just pour soup into the bowls and try not to fall behind," she said. Then she turned to Magnific. "You wanna be next to him?"

"That sounds splendid," Magnific said, handing me an apron. He had his tied around his waist already.

The day's menu featured creamy yellow squash soup, along with a salad, a brownie square, and an apple. The smell made my mouth water.

Lydia opened the doors and said hello to every person who walked through.

Volunteering at a soup kitchen isn't high on my list

of cool stuff to do before I die. Actually, it wasn't on it at all. My list had stuff like indoor skydiving, doing a flip on a trampoline, and riding an ostrich (yes, it's a thing), but as I handed out food to all the hungry people who had no place to go, I realized something. . . .

I've never been hungry before.

I mean, yeah, I've been *hungry*, but I could always eat something to fix that. I'm not sure any of the people there could just up and do something like that.

I felt *something*, but I wasn't sure what that something was, y'know what I mean? Like, suddenly I cared about people I'd never met before? Not just the people in front of me, but all the people in the world who didn't have food, either.

People I'd *never* even meet.

I felt sad for them.

All of them.

At the same freakin' time.

And even with my new abilities, I was powerless.

It was a lot for a twelve-year-old to take in.

Magnific nudged me with his elbow. "You okay, chum? You've stopped the soup."

THIS IS WHAT AN EXISTENTIAL CRISIS → LOOKS LIKE

He was right. All there was were empty bowls and a traffic jam in front of me. My existential crisis had glitched my brain for a minute.

"Sorry," I said, holding a bowl out to the woman waiting in front of me.

She smiled softly as she took it. "Thank you."

Magnific and I spent the next twenty minutes serving the rest of the line, but when we were done, I rushed out the doors to be alone. Or, as alone as I could be with the alien squid on my head.

I had to get out of there, not because I hated it, but because it was too much. Too overwhelming. Too real.

I climbed up to the roof and looked at the spot in the sky where the North Star would've been if it were dark out.

Nix said he couldn't read my mind, but I had my doubts, especially when he said, "The North Star. Your people call it Polaris. It's the brightest star in the constellation of Ursa Minor and it's about 433 light-years from here, unless you have a jump drive, which my ship does."

"How do you know so much about that star?" I asked.

"Because it's my home," Nix said. "Well, it's the *star* to my home. It's my sun. My family is there, and they're waiting for me."

How crazy was it that the star I'd been looking at every night for the past two years was the Reaper's home?

Fate.

Not coincidence.

"You don't want to destroy our world?"

"*No.*"

"I believe you," I said.

"*I know you do.*"

"I'll help you find your ship. I'll help you get home."

"*I know you will.*"

Did the Reaper and I just become friends? Because it seemed like the Reaper and I just became friends.

Magnific climbed the side of the building and joined me on the roof. He brought some bowls of creamy yellow squash soup for us, which I happily scarfed down. I was so hungry that Magnific let me eat his bowl, too.

It was about six p.m., and I had two hours before the Abandoned Children attacked. I should've been itching to get away to practice my powers, but to my surprise, I wasn't. In fact, it was kind of the opposite—I didn't want to leave.

"You deserve a trophy," Magnific said. "Best. Sidekick. Ever."

"Uh, thanks," I said. "But I still wish I could've used my powers for *something*."

Magnific chuckled. "I used to be just like you," he said nostalgically. "I used to want to fight crime all night long."

"What stopped you?" I asked.

"I realized that's what the police are for," Magnific said. "And it's more important for me to help those in need. The people downstairs, they don't need a strong guy; they need love."

"But what's the point of having a superpower if you never use it?"

Magnific stared at the sky. "Exactly."

"Don't you ever have days when you just want to use your superstrength?"

Magnific looked at me quizzically. "Superstrength?"

"Yeah," I said. "Your power."

He laughed abruptly. "I do *not* have superstrength, my funny friend!"

"Wait, what? No," I said. "But what about your jacked muscles?"

"I work out," Magnific said, proudly.

"But you picked me up like I was nothing!"

"Because I work out," he said again.

"If superstrength isn't your power, then what is?"

He leaned toward me and made sure nobody was looking. "I can turn into a shark," he whispered.

Then he did just that.

He turned into a giant shark.

We sat on the roof for another hour, just talking about random things. Everything inside me that wanted a superhero adventure was gone. I knew I'd be back at the academy soon enough, but for that short time on the roof, all I wanted to do was hang out with my new friend.

Nix loved it, too. He still kept himself invisible on my head, but I could tell he had become Magnific's number one fan.

When seven thirty rolled around, Magnific was trying to pack as much juicy knowledge into my brain as possible before I had to leave.

"Good grammar is *essential*," he said. "Never be late to anything, *ever*. Righty tighty, lefty loosey. Tostados are just lazy tacos—*don't let anybody tell you otherwise*. And finally, don't *ever* ask a woman if she's pregnant, *especially* if she *looks* pregnant—they don't like that."

"Got it," I said, tossing out a thumbs-up. "I hope I'll see you again, someday."

"I'm sure our paths will cross again," he said, patting me on the back one last time, trying to keep himself from crying. It was a *they-grow-up-so-fast* Hallmark moment. "You'll make a fine hero, Ben Braver. A fine one, indeed."

"If I'm anything like you, then it's pretty much guaranteed, right?" I said.

Magnific gasped, then bit his knuckle to keep his emotions in check. "Go, friend! Spread your wings and fly, little bird! Be the light in the dark!"

I nodded at Magnific, and then I took to the skies, faster than a speeding bullet.

I had a school to save.

CHAPTER TWENTY-TWO

8 p.m.

Minutes until the attack.

I zoomed over the interstate, following road signs to Lost Nation, the town near Kepler Academy.

I had flown from the moon to Earth in seconds, but in space there was nothing to crash into. I had to be a little more careful flying around on the planet.

My trip from Portland to Lost Nation took about thirty minutes. That's *fast*, but not fast enough—I was cutting it *way* too close.

The Abandoned Children attacked a little after eight p.m., which meant it was gonna happen pretty much the second I got there.

I saw the lights of Lost Nation, then looked up at the side of the mountain where Kepler Academy stood peacefully. It hadn't started yet.

Sailing silently through the night sky, I picked a spot in the forest, not too close, but not too far away, and then I dove straight down, performing the coolest superhero landing in all history.

As the dust settled, I scanned the area to make sure I was alone.

I wondered if Penny, Noah, and Donnie were nearby. They weren't gonna be too happy that I'd disappeared on them for half the day.

And how the heck was I gonna explain Nix to them? It's not like I could say, *"Oh, hey, the Reaper's not who we thought, and he's on my head right now. But he's cool, guys. He's cool."*

No way! They'd think he'd taken control of my brain and was *making* me say all that!

Suddenly, I heard footsteps crunching on dead leaves behind me. I spun around, but I was too late.

Whoever it was punched me so hard that my body tore through tree trunks like they were paper. If I didn't have Nix's powers, that punch would've killed me, for sure.

It *had* to be that lizard-dude, Matthew. The Abandoned Children must've been hiding in the forest waiting, and now I messed up the timeline by getting into a fight with them *before* they hit the school!

Matthew ran at me a second time. I got to my feet, ready for round two. If I could dodge his next punch, I could land one of my own, and then we'd see how strong I really was.

I clenched my fists as the lizard got closer, but then I realized I was totally wrong. It *wasn't* Matthew who was on me.

It was Noah.

He swung his fist and nailed me in the chest, a stream

of fire behind his elbow turning his normal punch into a *jet-packed* punch.

I flew back like a cannonball until I finally rolled to a stop.

Everything was spinning when I saw Penny out of the corner of my eye. I tried telling her to stop but couldn't get the words out because that's when she smashed a log over my head.

"Owwwww!" Nix and I cried out together.

With her skin glowing, she hoisted her log high above her for a second shot at me but stopped. "Ben?"

Just then, Donnie appeared out of nowhere and smashed his own log over my head.

"*STOP THAT!*" I shouted, clutching my precious skull, wondering how many brain cells I had left. "*It's me! Ben!*"

Noah ran up to us, holding a ball of fire in his hands. His jaw dropped when he saw me.

"Bro, we thought you were the Reaper!" he said.

"Wait, I hit you with *everything* I had. It should've *killed* you."

"*Don't tell them about me!*" Nix said in my head.

"Right," I said to Noah, "maybe next time wait to see who you're fighting before going for the kill shot."

Penny's glow disappeared as she fell to her knees, hugging me tightly. Her eyes were swollen and red. "But you're okay! After you disappeared, I wanted to get help from Headmaster Archer, but this fool wouldn't let me!" she said, pointing at Noah.

"Because we can't mess up this timeline!" Noah said like he was in charge. "Small changes mean big consequences! *After* the Abandoned Children attack and our old selves go back in time, we can do *whatever* we want, but until then, we have to stay hidden."

"Who died and made you boss?" I joked.

"*You* did," Noah said. "At least we *thought* you did."

Penny sniffled but nodded with a smile.

That's why her eyes were so swollen.

She'd been crying all day.

"Awww!" I said to her.

"Shut up," she said, pinching her fingers together.

Donnie plopped down next to me. "We figured you died *or* got taken over by the Reaper."

They had no idea how close to the truth they were.

"Where've you been?" Penny asked.

"Portland," I said honestly.

They stared blankly at me.

"Sooo, after I dropped you," Noah said, "you landed in Portland?"

"Nooo," I said. "I landed on the moon."

"Riiight," Penny said, putting her hand on mine. "And are you on the moon right now? If you are, it's time to come back to Earth, okay, buddy?"

"I'm not crazy!" I said.

"I never said that," Penny said in that tone of voice people use when they talk to someone they think is crazy.

"Can I just tell them?" I asked Nix. ". . . But they're my friends. It'll be fine. . . . No, seriously, it'll be okay. They're not gonna *hurt* you. . . . Whatever, yes, the log thing hurt, but they're not gonna do that again!"

"You're losing your grip, dude," Noah said.

"I'm fine!" I said to Noah, and then went back to Nix. "So you're cool with it? . . . Good . . . Yes, I promise! Just introduce yourself."

"Dude, what . . . ?" Penny said, suspicious.

I held my hands up, surrendering. "You guys, don't freak out, but . . ."

Nix unsuctioned himself off my head with a gross *SPLORTCH!*, and then became visible again.

Donnie freaked, punching me in the nose.

"Augh! Come on, man!" I said, stars swirling around my head.

"You're the Reaper!" he said.

Penny's skin radiated energy as she stumbled backward. Noah flinched as fire blazed up his arm. He pointed his fists at me.

Noah's chest heaved as the flames petered down. "He got you!"

"No!" I said. "I mean, kind of, but I let him! He's not the bad guy we thought he was!"

"Yeah, I'm not the bad guy!" Nix said.

"He's *making* you say that!" Penny said. Her arms

beaded with tiny drops of energy that fell, fizzling out in midair. "That's what he does! He latches on and takes control!"

"But that's not what's happening!" I said. "We're working together!"

"Obviously, you'd think that!" Noah said. "Because *that's* what he's *making* you think! You're under his control!"

But . . . I wasn't.

Was I?

"Everybody be cool," Nix said, trying to calm everyone down.

Donnie punched me in the face again.

Just then, thunder cracked in the sky. The wind went from zero to sixty almost instantly. Dead leaves and pine needles ripped through the forest toward the school. Trees weren't getting blown around; they were getting sucked up.

The earth shook as we ran.

When we got to the edge of the forest, nobody said a word.

We didn't have to.

We all knew what was going on.

It was the Abandoned Children.

And their attack on Kepler Academy had begun.

CHAPTER TWENTY-THREE

The five of us watched William tear apart the front of the academy using his vortex of doom. He controlled it perfectly, twisting and bending it, waving his arms like he was the maestro of a hard-core orchestra.

Delilah and Matthew stood back, letting William do his thing. I could even see Victoria behind all of them now that I was outside.

Penny's arms glowed brightly as tiny beads of energy formed on her skin. It was definitely one way of wearing her emotions on her sleeve.

She flinched when I took her hand. She inhaled deeply and then smiled at me. "Sorry," she said.

I don't know if she noticed her glow disappear when she smiled, but I sure did.

"Here's the plan," Noah said. "We don't move a muscle until our past selves are gone, then we surprise-attack William and his buddies from behind."

"But the lizard-dude won't be with them," I said. "Remember? He chased us into the lab."

"You guys got a lab?" Nix said out loud from the top of my noggin. "What do you need a lab for?"

"Dude, shut him up," Noah said, upset.

"It doesn't work like that," I said.

Nix made a face and plopped himself back on my head, turning invisible again.

"I hate the idea of doing nothing while they attack," Penny said.

"But we can't interfere," Noah said. "That could mess up what's supposed to happen."

"So we don't go to the lobby," Penny said. "We can do *other* things, like get *ready* to fight instead of *waiting* to fight."

Noah looked at Penny. "Are you even gonna do anything? You don't have your powers anymore."

"I still *have* them," Penny snipped. "I'm just not *using* them. But you don't need powers to punch someone in the face."

"Wait," I said, feeling the juices in my brain bubble up an idea. Noah's comment about not having powers . . . "You guys! We need the Power Dampener!"

"My dad's crossbow?" Donnie said. "But that's back in 1963. I guess I could go get it and—"

"NO!" Noah said. "No more time travel!"

"We don't *need* to time-travel for it!" I said. "I bet it's still somewhere in the school! There's no way he would've thrown something like that away."

"If it's here, then why haven't we seen it in the past two years?" Noah asked. "Why didn't someone use it on Abigail? Or Angel?"

"I don't know," I said, "but you saw Duncan's lab last year—it was a hot mess. This school doesn't do a great job of keeping things like that organized. And if anyone would know where it is, it'd be Duncan. We gotta find him."

"Who's Duncan?" Donnie asked.

"He's a ghost teacher," Penny said. "Ben killed him last year."

"He was *already* dead!" I said.

"*Cooool*," Donnie said.

The five of us looked down at the lobby from the edge of the forest. William was just wrapping things up, closing his fists and making his tornado thing disappear. He and the other Abandoned Children made their way inside the broken lobby, leaving Victoria out front to keep watch.

Duncan was hiding in the coffee shop with our past selves. We needed to get down there and get his attention.

Noah took the lead as we followed, keeping low to the ground. When we got to the side of the building, we hid behind some rubble. I peeked over the edge to watch what I'd seen earlier that day.

Headmaster Archer was in the lobby, confronting William and his goons.

Archer said nothing.

"Really? The silent treatment is gonna get you no-where."

We crawled along the edge of the school and ducked under one of the shattered windows on the side of the building.

The back of the coffee shop was in perfect view. I saw myself and my friends hiding behind the counter with Totes and Dexter. Duncan was floating beside them.

"How do we get his attention?" Penny asked.

"We could throw some rocks at him," I said, already chucking a handful of pebbles through the window.

Noah grabbed my wrist and pulled me back. "Are you an idiot? Throwing rocks is gonna get *everybody's* attention! We only want *Duncan's*."

Noah was right.

I needed to think before acting.

We looked inside, hoping I didn't mess things up.

The other Ben was cupping his hands over his face. Everyone else was looking up, afraid the building was about to crumble apart. Then I remembered getting pelted by pebbles earlier and how much it hurt.

I did it to myself.

Maybe I *am* an idiot.

All I needed to do was get Duncan to look at us one time. If he saw two versions of us, then he'd connect the dots and come over.

But he just wasn't looking. He was too concerned with what was going on in the lobby.

I had to do something fast because we were running out of time. In just a few seconds, Dexter was gonna wake up and start freaking out. All heck was about to break loose.

I stood up straight, trying to get into Duncan's line of sight, but hoping Victoria and the Abandoned Children couldn't see me, and then I started waving my arms in the air.

Duncan was in the middle of giving our past selves instructions about sneaking down to the lab. He was totally oblivious to me.

So Noah, Penny, and Donnie joined in with the waving, and finally, Duncan turned slightly, like something had caught his eye.

It worked.

He said one last thing to our past selves and then flew into the floor, disappearing. The past version of Penny in the coffee shop started panicking, taking quick breaths and squeezing her hands with her fingers.

Duncan reappeared in front of us with a scalding look on his face. Then he sighed. "I'd ask how this is possible, but I see that Donnie is with you. If this were *any* other circumstance, I'd be upset, but . . . I'm just glad to know you'll make it out of that coffee shop alive."

"Oh, okay," Penny said. "I get why you left us back there now."

We took off around the building until we were completely out of sight of the lobby, and without any time to explain, I just dove right in. "We need Richard Kepler's Power Dampener! Do you know where it is?"

"The what?" Duncan said.

"It's like a weird-looking crossbow that shoots a glowing net," Penny said.

"My dad made it," Donnie said proudly.

"What's it do?" Duncan asked.

"The net takes away someone's power," I said.

"Yep, that'd be pretty nice to have right about now," Duncan said as he flew down the side of the school. "I've never seen anything like that, but follow me!"

I groaned, trying to keep up with the fast-flying ghost as Penny, Noah, and Donnie trailed behind us.

Duncan went on as we rushed through the backyard of Kepler Academy. "That doesn't mean it's *not* here somewhere," he said, hopeful. "If I've got it, then it would be in storage."

"In the lab?" I said.

"No," Duncan said. "It would've been on the rooftop shed with all my other stuff."

"But the shed's not on the roof anymore," I said.

"Right," Duncan said, slowing as we approached a small wooden building pushed up against the back of the school. "But everything from *that* shed's been moved into *this* shed."

We shielded our eyes as Noah blasted the doors open with a fiery explosion.

Duncan sighed. "The doors weren't locked, buddy."

"Oh, sorry," Noah said, embarrassed. "It's just, we're in a hurry, and uh . . ."

"Yeah, I get it," Duncan said.

We tore through every box in that shed, leaving nothing untouched, but the Power Dampener wasn't there.

It was gone.

"I'm not surprised," Duncan said. "I don't think there's anything here from the first year. Everything's been tossed out or replaced."

The building trembled again as another explosion came from the front of the school.

William and his goons had started their second attack.

And we still didn't know what to do.

CHAPTER TWENTY-FOUR

The past versions of me, Penny, and Noah were getting chased by Matthew through the school. In just a few minutes, they'd escape to the past, and we'd be caught up with the timeline.

Richard's bomb-diggity Power Dampener would've been supes helpful—actually, it would've completely saved the day—but we didn't have it.

I looked at Penny as the sounds of battle shook the school. This was the real deal. We could get hurt out there. We could even *die*. And I couldn't let that happen to her.

I mean, her *and* Noah.

Obviously, I didn't want Noah to die, either, but Penny's *Penny*. She's . . . you know what I mean.

Luckily, we had something *better* than the Power Dampener.

We had *me*.

Nix gave me powers. *Big* powers. Superstrength and superspeed. I just needed to fly in fast, bust some heads, tie 'em up, and the day would be saved, right?

My friends wouldn't get hurt.

William, Delilah, and Matthew would be caught. Heck, I bet they'd even fess up and tell us where the rest of the Abandoned Children were! It was such a simple solution that I couldn't believe I was even questioning it.

I needed to be a lone wolf.

I took a deep breath and floated off the ground.

Duncan's jaw dropped.

"Ben, wait!" Noah said. "We need a plan!"

"There's no time for plans," I said, feeling Nix's power flow through my body.

"*Yesss!*" Nix said in my head. "*It's showtime!*"

"You guys need to take cover in the forest," I said to my friends. "Keep Donnie hidden, and don't come out until it's safe!"

Noah and Duncan tried to stop me, but their words faded as I flew into the school.

I headed to the secret tunnel under the academy. At that point in the battle, Matthew was for sure trying to break into the lab.

I zigged and zagged through the halls and swooped down flights of stairs until I was finally staring at the lab at the other end of the tunnel.

It was only seconds after our past selves had escaped.

Matthew tore through the laboratory, trying to find the kids who were just in there. His grunts echoed down the empty hall.

"*This is it,*" Nix said. "*Don't get scared. Don't freeze up. You got this.*"

"I got this," I said, and then I shouted, "Hey, you, dragon-butt!"

From twenty feet away, the lizard peered out the door at me. He snapped his jaw, snarling as he crawled out on all fours, cautiously, keeping his eyes glued to mine. He was slowly closing the gap between us.

My heart raced like crazy.

Matthew continued to stare me down. I wasn't sure what he was thinking, but it was probably something along the lines of "*Kill, kill, kill, kill, kill . . .*"

I needed to say something.

Superheroes always say cool things before a battle.

Something smart. Clever. Quippy.

"*Yum, yum, gimme some!*" I shouted, then cringed at myself. "Great, thanks a lot, Totes."

Matthew shot forward at lightning speed. He was so fast that I didn't even have time to think. I acted on instinct, bringing my hands up to protect my face.

Good thing, too, because he was trying to bite it off.

"You have superstrength, but you're not invincible!" Nix reminded me.

In other words—I couldn't mess around.

I struggled under the lizard, imagining Nix's camouflaged tentacles wrapping around the monster.

The lizard panicked as all eight invisible, wormy limbs slithered over his scaly green skin. He tried to fight back, but he was no match. Within seconds, I had him wrapped up like a McDonald's breakfast burrito.

I won!

My first battle was a success.

Not that I had any doubts, but y'know . . .

With Matthew as my prisoner, I flew back to the front of the school, where the bigger battle was still raging.

Archer and Totes were defending themselves inside the school as William and Delilah pressed forward.

William was a pro with his power, opening and closing perfectly placed vortexes to hurl large chunks of broken concrete exactly where he wanted them to go.

Bolts of electricity streamed from Delilah's fingertips like she was the Emperor from *Star Wars*.

Surprisingly, Vic and Dexter weren't in the fight. They were hiding behind the rubble.

Archer was on the defensive, doing everything he

could to keep himself and Totes from getting crushed or electrocuted, but they were backed into a corner. They were about to lose.

Ben Braver to the rescue.

I hovered over the battle, dangling the lizard down in front of everyone with Nix's invisible tentacles.

The look on Vic's face was priceless. It looked like we had the same power of levitation since Matthew was basically floating under me.

The chaos screeched to a halt when William used a vortex to seal Archer and Totes in the corner with a chunk of broken concrete.

I hoped they were okay.

"Wait, wait, wait!" William shouted, making a T shape with his hands. *"Time-out!"*

All eyes were on me when I landed in the middle of the lobby.

"Well, *look* at you! Ben Braver, in the flesh!" William said, applauding. He glanced back at Delilah like she should clap, too, but she didn't.

William knew me?

I guess it wasn't too crazy.

I *did* save the school once.

Maybe twice.

Matthew wiggled free from Nix's tentacles, and then he scurried behind his evil buddies.

William approached me, holding his hand out. I stepped back, until I realized he only wanted a handshake.

I didn't know what to do.

My goal was to stop the battle, and I had, but I didn't plan on what to do *after* that.

THE NAME'S WILLIAM WOLFF. IT'S AN HONOR TO MEET YOU, MY DUDE!

William spun in a circle with his arms out. "You're the *hero* of Kepler Academy. Every descendant knows your name! *My parents* even know who you are! You know, there's a whole lot of folks who believe you're the Chosen One?"

"Chosen for what?" I asked.

William shrugged with a pout. "I don't know. Lead them? Save them? Make a world where we don't have to hide anymore? You've gone against *everything* the academy stands for, but you're not punished for it like the rest of us would be. Nope. You're seen as a hero, and you don't even have a power! BTW, how *can* you fly?"

Nix's paranoid voice came from inside my brain. *"Don't tell him about me!"*

"Very carefully," I answered.

"Fine," he said with a suspicious smile. "Keep your secrets."

I wasn't 100 percent sure what William was doing, but I think he was trying to monologue. Abigail did it. Angel did it. Why would he be any different?

But monologues are a trick. They distract the hero from saving the day, and I couldn't let that happen.

Nix thought the same thing. *"He's stalling,"* he said in my head. *"He's sizing you up as he speaks."*

"Surrender!" I commanded. "It's over for you and your cronies."

William glanced at Delilah, like, *"Is he serious?"*

She shrugged her shoulders and rolled her eyes.

"Look, you're just a kid," William said, "so I don't want to hurt you. We came here for one thing. Once we get it, we'll leave."

"You'll never find Donnie," I said.

That got his attention. His jaw twitched as he stared at me.

I continued. "Besides, even if you *did* get him, there's no way he'd join you. He's *not* a villain."

William looked at me sympathetically. He put his hand on my shoulder. "Ohhhh," he said. "You've got it all wrong, little dude. We don't want him to join the Abandoned Children."

A hundred reasons for kidnapping Donnie came to mind, but only one stuck out.

The most horrible one.

I didn't say it out loud because it was too dark.

Too real.

"Then why do you want him?" I asked.

William squeezed my shoulder tight.

CHAPTER TWENTY-FIVE

William punched me square in the face.

Back in Portland, I barely felt a whole car *crash into me*, but for some reason, William's punch hurt like bajankers.

"Not the face!" Nix groaned in my head. *"We're weak if I get hit like that!"*

William pounded his knuckles on the side of my head, over and over, and I could feel my connection with Nix slipping.

I stumbled back. "You said you weren't gonna hurt me!"

"No," William said, landing a solid blow to my tummy. "I said I didn't *want* to hurt you—but I totally will if I *have* to."

I keeled over in pain. I was dizzy. I couldn't breathe. And I was trying desperately not to barf up yellow squash soup.

Why did I eat so much of it??

William pinned me down with his knee on my head, right on top of Nix. I heard the alien scream in my skull.

"Where's Donnie?" William asked as he curled his fingers, opening a minivortex next to my face that sucked at my cheeks. "You know, I have no idea what's on the other side of these things? Do *you* want to find out?"

I tried moving Nix's tentacles, but William's knee was doing a number on our bond. Nix was trying to say something, but his words were a jumbled mess of random sounds.

"Give me what I want," William said. "That kid's a time traveler. Abigail told us all about it—that Headmaster Kepler changed history, but that's such a cheater move!"

"*Donnie* didn't do that! That was the old man, and he's already dead!"

"They're the *same person!*" William laughed as he stood up. "And as long as Donnie's around, he can stop us before we ever do anything! With *both* Headmaster Kepler and Donnie dead, we can do whatever we please, and we please to take over the world!"

"That'll never happen!" Noah said, suddenly dropping down out of nowhere. His hands burst into flames as he powered up.

Penny ran out from behind the rubble with a battle cry and another log over her head.

GET AWAY FROM MY FRIENDS!

It was game-on.

These fools were gonna feel the full force of what my friends and I could do, even if Penny wasn't using her powers.

And with William's knee off my alien buddy, Nix was back in my head. *"You don't have to kill him, but can you please shut him up?"*

No time for smart-aleck comments—just action.

I used Nix's tentacles to spring up from the ground, and then I shot them forward at William. Noah aimed his fists at William as Penny closed in behind him.

But we weren't fast enough.

Delilah had him covered.

Her lightning bolts raged through our bodies, sending us flying in different directions.

Then she jolted me a second time after I hit the ground, maybe to teach me a lesson, I don't know.

Electricity surged through me as I flew back at a hundred miles per hour. My muscles strained, and my bones felt like they were about to snap.

Nix's tentacles wrapped around me, and then I heard his voice in the back of my head. *"This is gonna hurt me more than it hurts you!"*

I smashed against one of the last standing walls in the lobby. It was all shattered glass, protruding nails, and splintered wood. Nix's tentacles shielded me from all that.

Then I fell flat on the ground, totally paralyzed.

All I could do was watch.

Delilah cracked her knuckles, like "no big deal," like she hadn't just tried to kill three children.

Noah and Penny were out cold.

Archer and Totes were still trapped in the corner.

Duncan floated silently above it all. He would've helped if he could. I know he would've.

We were no match for the Abandoned Children.

They schooled us like it was nothing.

Victoria took orders from William as Dexter stood behind her with a pale face.

Then William took Penny's limp body, dragging her across the floor as Victoria used her powers to push the rubble out of their way.

"Stop!" I shouted, but it was only a whisper. Then I tried talking to Nix. *"Nix . . . I need your help. . . ."*

But he didn't say anything.

He wasn't on my head anymore.

The Abandoned Children gathered together. Matthew hoisted Penny's body over his shoulder as she whimpered. At least I knew she was still alive.

Everything was shifting in and out of focus, and suddenly William was kneeling by my side. I tried grabbing him, but he took my hand and gently laid it on my chest.

"I know how much you love comics," William said, smiling. "Like, that's your thing, right? So check this— I'm gonna do what a comic book villain would do because it sounds *fun*."

William was a psycho.

"We're taking your girlfriend," he said. "And if you want to see her alive again, bring us Donnie."

I opened my mouth, but he pressed his finger against my lips. "Shhhh," he said. "There's nothing more to say. Either *Donnie* dies or *she* does. The choice is yours. You've got *one* hour."

With the roof of the lobby gone, the North Star silently twinkled above. It was just a dot in the sky, but it felt like a disappointed dad that just watched his son fail at life.

I was selfish. Stupid. Greedy. And everything was messed up again because of it. I thought superpowers were supposed to *FIX* all that!

I wanted to be brave for my friends. For my mom. For my dad. I didn't want to show William that I was afraid. I tried to fight the ugly cry, but I couldn't do it.

The tears were already flowing.

William wiped my wet cheeks clean with his thumb. "Hey, it'll be okay," he said. "I *swear* I won't hurt her as long as you bring us Donnie. One hour."

An hour wasn't enough time.

I wasn't even sure I'd be able to stand again in an hour.

"Most villains give at *least* twenty-four hours," I rasped.

William chuckled. "There he is," he said. "Fine. Then you have *two* hours."

"Where do I find you?"

"I'll let you know," he said as he walked back to his crew. "Time to go!" he shouted.

William, Delilah, Matthew, and Vic huddled together, but Dexter didn't budge from his spot across the lobby.

"What're you waiting for?" Victoria asked.

Dexter didn't say anything.

"C'mon, Dex," she said, almost pleading.

Dexter stared hard at the floor and shook his head.

"Leave him," William said. "If he doesn't give himself to the Abandoned Children, then he's against us."

There was a flash of light, and they were gone.

I don't know how they disappeared, but that wasn't important. What *was* important was that Penny was in trouble. I needed to trade Donnie's life for hers, but there was no way I could do that, right?

Not like it really mattered.

Because when I looked up, I saw Donnie come out from some rubble he was hiding behind. He had been there the whole time. He heard everything William said, and he knew they wanted him dead.

He looked at me for a moment, like he was trying to figure out what to do. And then he sank into the floor, saving himself by going Outside.

He totally bailed on us.

CHAPTER TWENTY-SIX

█ messed up.

My lone-wolf attitude had almost killed me and Noah, and it got Penny kidnapped. So much for being an all-amazing superhero.

I crawled across the floor, searching for Nix. We must've gotten split up when we smashed into the wall.

Totes finally dug Headmaster Archer and himself out from the corner. Archer's leg was clearly broken, but he acted like it was fine. Duncan tried to persuade him to go down to the Lost Nation hospital, but he refused, so Totes found an old pair of crutches from the nurse's office.

Dexter was by Noah's side, helping him get his strength back with a soda and some muffins he found in the trashed coffee shop.

I pushed some rubble aside and kept looking for the alien squid. He *had* to be here somewhere. Hopefully he wasn't badly hurt, or worse, *dead*.

"Ben, *what* are you doing?" Duncan called out from across the lobby.

I almost lied to him, but with less than two hours to save Penny, I didn't have time. So I was completely honest. "I'm looking for an alien!"

Duncan paused. "Don't play!" he said.

"I'm not!" I said, sliding my hands across the floor.

And then I found him.

Nix.

He was a pathetic lump of flesh, covered in dust. His limbs had huge gashes in them—some so deep that the tentacle was barely still attached. I carefully scooped him up in my hands. His body was like a ball of slime, his arms drooping over the sides of my palms. I begged him to say something, anything, but he didn't.

He wasn't breathing.

But honestly, I wasn't sure if he *needed* to breathe.

Headmaster Archer limped over on his crutches, grunting the whole way as Duncan floated behind him.

"What in the world is *that*?" Archer whispered.

THAT'S HIM, ISN'T IT?

HIM? YOU MEAN THAT'S -- THAT'S THE REAPER?

"What're you doing with him?" Duncan asked scoldingly. "Why's he even here?"

"He came back when Donnie fell on the stage,"

I said, cradling the squid in my hands, careful not to stretch his slippery body in a weird way. "He's not who you think he is."

"He's the reason Kepler changed history," Archer said. "He's the reason the world ended."

"No, he's not!" I said. "When Kepler changed things, Nix didn't have the chance to destroy the world. He was trapped Outside the whole time. This version of Nix hasn't done *anything* wrong!"

"*I* didn't name him; his *name* is Nix," I said. "He saved my life when we hit the wall, and I think he's dying because of it."

"Good!" Duncan said.

I stood, gently holding the alien squid. "He's the only reason I'm alive right now! He doesn't want to hurt anybody! He just wanted me to help him find his ship so he could go home! He *just* wants to go home!"

Duncan looked at me, astonished, but speechless.

I pleaded with the ghost. "You gotta believe me. Have I ever done anything that would make me untrustworthy?"

"Yes!" Duncan said immediately. "Like, a thousand times, yes!"

"If he wanted to hurt anybody, he would've done it already," I said. "Penny's in trouble, but *he* can help us get her back! You *have* to just trust me! Please!"

Noah staggered over. "Penny doesn't have time," he said. "And we need all the help we can get. I don't even care if that thing is good or bad—if it gives Ben powers, then we can use them to get her back."

"Thanks," I said.

"Nope," my friend said without looking at me. "I'm doing this for Penny. Not you."

Duncan and Archer looked at each other the same way my parents do when they're about to agree to something they don't want to.

"We don't have *any* other options," Archer said.

Duncan sighed, nodding. He looked at the limp squid in my hands. "We need to get him down to the lab."

A few minutes later, the seven of us were making our way through the secret tunnel under the school. I held Nix in my arms, hoping it wasn't too late for him.

The lab door must've shut on its own after Matthew's attack because it was closed when we got there. I stepped forward so the biometric scanner could see me, but the door slid open before I even got close.

"Did it scan me?" I asked, cradling Nix like a baby.

"Nope," Duncan said.

"Then how'd it open?"

Duncan didn't answer that one.

The walls inside lit up brighter than I'd ever seen before. Even the *outside* walls seemed to come alive.

Something *different* was happening.

One by one, we walked in.

The lab had always been a quiet place with a few holograms on the wall, but now it looked like we were standing inside a video game. The hologram interfaces followed our every move. One of the interfaces even tracked my eye movement, keeping some images in front of me wherever I looked. Walls were moving, shifting slightly, almost like the room was breathing.

"What is this place?" Dexter asked.

"Duncan's secret lab," I said, and then I bragged a little. "I've been coming here for about a year now."

When I got to the middle of the room, the holograms on the sidewall switched from green to red, with flashing icons all over the place, followed by a small, beeping alarm.

Everyone jumped as a black metal wall buzzed next to us. Invisible seams appeared, transforming into a little operating table as tiny robotic arms slid out.

Above the table was a three-dimensional image of

Nix, with the damaged parts of his body highlighted. I knew what it all meant—Nix was in critical condition.

He wasn't dead, but he was dying.

"Quickly, Ben," Duncan said. "Put him on the table."

I gently set Nix on the black metal, and the robotic arms automatically went to work on him.

Everybody gathered behind me to watch.

"This isn't a lab, is it?" I asked, never looking away from the alien on the operating table.

"Nope," Duncan said.

"If it's not a lab," Noah said, "then what is it?"

The holograms danced on the walls around us. The room had never come to life the same way it had when Nix entered.

It *knew* who he was.

It was built for *him* . . . the alien squid.

And then everything was suddenly so clear to me.

CHAPTER TWENTY-SEVEN

Noah, Totes, Dexter, and I were in the school kitchen digging through the pantry. Nix had been on the operating table for about forty-five minutes. Nobody knew how long it takes for robots to fix an alien, so Archer volunteered to wait in the lab in case there was any progress.

Snacks would've been a nice distraction, but I wasn't hungry. There was less than an hour until William's deadline, and if Nix wasn't better soon, we'd have to go without him.

Dexter flipped on a TV in the corner.

"Are you missing your show or something?" Totes asked.

"No," Dexter said. "I just can't stand all the quiet. Makes my head feel like it's gonna pop."

Noah skimmed through Kepler Academy yearbooks that he had fetched from the library. He was hoping to figure out where Donnie had gone.

"Did you know Donnie's parents disappeared, too?" Noah said. "Only a month after the school opened?"

"Yeah," I said. "I remember that."

That's when Duncan showed up.

"Remember what?" he asked.

"That Donnie's parents disappeared, too," I said.

"Ah, yes," Duncan said. "The story is, after their son vanished, they went off the radar to search for him."

"But they *knew* where he went," Noah said.

Duncan arched his brow at Noah.

I jumped in to change the subject. "What're we gonna do about Penny?"

Duncan shook his head. "The truth is, I don't know what to do. This kind of thing was never planned for because Headmaster Kepler kept it all contained. It's all unraveling now that Donald's gone."

"We could call the cops," I suggested.

"And say what?" Totes asked. "That a man who can open funnels of dark energy kidnapped a little girl who's a walking atom bomb? And that they shouldn't be too hard to find since there's a giant *lizard* with them?"

The goat was right.

That'd be weird.

Like, *laughably* weird.

"I spent the day with a guy named Magnific," I said. "Maybe we can call him for help?"

"*Magnific*," Duncan repeated. "I know *exactly* who that is, and he's not the only one playing secret superhero. About a dozen have shown up in the past year.

They'd be a *huge* help, but they've made themselves impossible to find, and we've got less than an hour."

"I can't believe you don't have a secret team of superheroes to call just in case something like this happens," I said, frustrated. "Haven't you learned *anything* from the Avengers?"

"Uh, no," Duncan said like, "*Duh.*"

"Then *we* have to be that team," I said.

Noah suddenly slammed his hands on the table. "How can you talk about comics right now? Penny's in *real* trouble, dude! She's *seriously* gonna die if we can't help her! Maybe you could see that if you stopped being immature for a single hot second!"

Noah had been like that all day, and I was done with it. "What's your problem, man?"

"*You're* my problem!" he shouted. "*None* of this would've happened if you didn't go off on your own all the time!"

"You don't know that!" I said, even though he was probably right.

"You make things worse by doing whatever you want. Screwing things up is the only thing you're good at! *That's* your *real* power!"

"I was just trying to help!"

"Help *how*? We're supposed to have each other's back, but it doesn't work when you keep ditching us! That's not how a *team* works! You don't even care about the rest of us!"

"That's *why* I do things alone! Because I don't want any of you getting hurt!"

"No! You do it cuz you're a show-off!" Noah said, getting in my face. "You wanted powers so you could be a hero, but now that you have 'em, all you are is a stupid kid who can't do anything right!"

"No, I'm not!" I said, shoving Noah away from me.

That was a mistake.

Noah snapped and started throwing punches.

I'm not proud to say that I did, too.

Totes and Dexter pulled us away from each other.

"Dude, chill!" Dexter shouted, holding Noah back. "Ben screwed up, okay? Can we just forget it and move on?"

"What do *you* care?" Noah said, jerking away from Dexter. "You and Penny aren't even friends!"

"That doesn't mean I want her to *die!*" Dexter said. "And in case you forgot, Vic is in trouble, too, just like Penny!"

"Victoria made her choice," Totes said.

"No, she made a *mistake*," Dexter said, suddenly choking up. "I *know* she doesn't want to be there. I could hear it in her voice."

Nobody said anything.

Dexter sniffled. "All I'm sayin' is, if Vic were here, I'd be hugging her to death. I wouldn't waste time fighting with her because of a mistake she made."

Kudos to Dexter for bringing us all back to reality.

Noah finally looked at me.

"Sorry, bro," he said quietly.

"Me, too," I said. "We're *better* as a team, and I won't make that mistake again."

We bumped fists.

"So . . . we're a team, then?" Dexter asked.

Noah and I looked at each other and then back at Dexter. I held my fist up. Noah put his next to mine, and we both looked at Dexter, waiting for him to join.

He did.

A hairy hoof clapped down on top of our hands. "Me, too!" Totes screeched. "I'm part of the team, too! Don't like it? Fight me."

Everybody laughed.

The TV screen across the room flashed bright red with the words BREAKING NEWS IN TIMES SQUARE, NEW YORK CITY! scrolling across the top. Suspenseful music played as a shaky camera followed a news reporter running down the street.

We gathered around the small TV set to see what was happening.

"Good evening, Sara Conwell here with BNC News in Times Square, New York City, where three individuals have cleared out the area using supernatural abilities. One of the individuals appears to be wearing some sort of lizard costume that allows him to cling to the walls."

"Oh. My. Gecko," Duncan whispered.

Sara continued. "One of the individuals, a young woman, appearing to be in her early twenties, is somehow summoning electricity through her hands, perhaps by a glove of some sort. And the third individual is a man, also in his early twenties, creating dark tornadoes over the square. The how and why of these individuals is still unclear."

The camera panned from the reporter to William, Delilah, and Matthew in the background. Penny, too. William waved when he noticed he was being filmed, and then he ran toward the reporter.

"It appears that the young man is coming to greet us now," the reporter said.

As William approached, he turned away from the camera for a moment. "Is there anything in my teeth?" he asked Sara and then opened his mouth wide.

"No, no, you're fine," she said, and then faced the

screen again. "You're watching BNC News, where we've just made contact with the—"

William snatched the mic and pushed Sara aside, then he got *way* too close to the camera.

WE ARE THE **ABANDONED CHILDREN OF KEPLER ACADEMY**! AND WE'RE WAITING FOR YOU, **BEN BRAVER**! YOU'VE GOT **THIRTY MINUTES** TO GIVE US WHAT WE WANT!

William turned the mic sideways and dropped it on the ground.

"*Thirty minutes*," he mouthed dramatically.

Sara picked up the mic and looked at the camera. "*Who* are the Abandoned Children? And *who* is Ben Braver?"

Noah, Dexter, and Totes all looked at me.

"So . . . *that's* not good," I said.

"Those fools are using their powers on TV," Duncan sighed. "They said the *name* of the school."

"Plus *Ben's* name," Totes added.

My name was now scrolling at the top of the TV screen, along with the BREAKING NEWS! line. If Penny were there, she would've slapped my back and laughed about it.

"There's gonna be *hundreds* of cell phones in Times Square," Totes added. "Damage control is impossible. Our secret's out."

"But at least we know where Penny is," I said.

"Yeah, but we're in Colorado," Dexter said. "How are we gonna get to New York City in thirty minutes?"

He was right. That distance was too far. Even if I had Nix on my head, it would be cutting it close.

And that's when Duncan perked up.

CHAPTER TWENTY-EIGHT

We were all back in the lab, er, *spaceship.*

Nix was still on the operating table, but the lights above him had changed from a scary bloodred to a gentle, thirst-quenching blue.

Archer was propped up on crutches, standing next to the table. "He's feeling good enough to talk, Ben. He's been asking for you."

I slowly approached my alien buddy. "Thanks for saving my life, dude."

Nix smiled weakly. "Don't mention it, Beanie Weenie."

"Wait, why'd he call you that?" Noah asked, but I ignored him. "Ben? Ben, why'd he call you that?"

"I found your ship," I said to Nix with a shrug.

Nix exhaled slowly. "I can go home now."

I don't know if it was because of our E.T.-Elliott bond, or if it was because my face was as easy to read as a lying lion, but he knew something was off.

"But I'm not going just yet, am I?" Nix said, uneasy.

He was worried about getting imprisoned again by humans, I just knew it.

"No, you can!" I said. "It's just—we kind of, uhhh . . ."

"What?" Nix said weakly.

Dexter interrupted us. "We need a ride, Squidward."

"We have to get across the country in fifteen minutes," I explained. "If you're up for one more adventure before you go home, we could really use your ship to get there, and *I* could really use *your* help to—"

"Get the people who did this?" Nix said, finishing my sentence.

I nodded. "They took Penny. She's . . . one of my best friends."

Dexter smiled a sly smile. "C'mon . . . she's *just* a friend?" Then he made kissy lips.

Noah and Totes laughed, making the same sounds.

"Shut up," I said, and then I looked back at Nix. "Will you help me?"

Nix looked at me like, *"Duh, of course I will."*

He was so small and feeble. I hoped he *could* help.

"But I just need to rest a bit more," he said softly, rolling to his side and closing his eyes.

Archer walked to the door, his face pale and his hands shaking. He was in pretty bad shape, too. That's when I realized he wasn't coming with us.

"I don't suppose I can talk you out of this?" he asked. "You're only alive because William *let* you live. I guarantee he won't let you walk away from a second fight. *Any* of you."

I looked him straight in the eye. "We're going to get Penny back," I said like it was the only purpose to my life, which, at that moment, it was.

Noah and Dexter folded their arms as Totes huffed.

Archer knew we weren't messing around. He looked at Duncan. "Keep them safe."

"I'll do what I can," Duncan said.

And then Headmaster Archer walked out the door.

I went to the front of the ship.

Or at least what I *thought* was the front.

"Where the heck's the cockpit?" I asked.

"They're usually in front of the window," Duncan said. "But there are no windows in here."

"Then how do you work this thing?"

"Honestly, I don't know. I've never flown it."

"But how'd it get down here?"

"Probably a semi or something. It was here *long* before I was."

"But haven't you messed with it before? I figured you would have flown it all over the place by now!"

"Hey, everybody," Duncan said to the group. "Between me and Ben, who's the guy who's gonna irresponsibly play with technology he doesn't understand?"

"Ben," every single person in the room said at the same time, Nix included.

"Whatever," I said. "Nix, what do I do?"

But the squid had already fallen asleep again.

He woke up for half a second just to burn me.

Nice.

I waved my hand through different holographic interfaces, trying to make sense of everything. And then I came to a screen with a little Help icon, so like a noob, I clicked the icon.

A strange keyboard popped up on the display in front of me, like nothing I'd ever seen before. It was strange. Alien. Creepy, almost.

But you wanna hear something crazy?

I knew how to use it.

My fingers danced across the alien keys like they had little baby brains of their own. Different screens flashed in front of me, and I could even *read* the alien language.

It must've been a side effect from having Nix in my head all day.

How flippin' cool is that?

"So what's happening right now?" Duncan asked, eyeballing me suspiciously.

"I get this thing! Flying it is gonna be easier than I thought," I said. "All I have to do is punch in our destination, and the ship will take us there on autopilot."

A holographic map zeroed in on our location in the Colorado mountains, highlighting the ship with a red triangle. I chuckled because the writing under the triangle said YOU ARE HERE ... but it was in alien, so I was the only one who thought it was funny.

The map worked exactly like a map on a cell phone. I zoomed out until I found New York City, and then I zoomed in on Times Square. I circled it with my finger, slid to another screen, and poked the Launch button.

But nothing happened.

"That should've worked," I said.

"Maybe it's out of gas," Dexter said.

"Do alien ships use gas?" Totes asked.

"Doubt it," Duncan said. "This thing is just old. It probably hasn't flown since the forties. Are you sure you initiated the launch sequence correctly?"

"I mean, maybe?" I said, scanning the display for something I might've missed. And then I saw the reason we weren't moving. I pushed another button on the screen, feeling like an idiot. "The parking brake was on."

Noah burst out laughing.

I hit the Launch button again, and this time the ship fired up, creaking and cracking against the rock outside.

The black metal wall in front of me became blurry

and then completely disappeared. I could see the secret tunnel right outside the ship.

"It's transparent," Duncan said, delighted.

The ship shook loose from under the school and slowly crept upward through the rock of the mountain, but also through some of the school building, crumbling the lower part of the west wing.

"Sorry," I said, cringing.

Duncan winked at me. "It's not the first time you've destroyed part of the school."

The ship rose above Kepler Academy as the engines warmed up with clicks and clacks, making the same sounds a roller coaster does.

And then, without warning, in a smooth motion, the ship shot straight for the stars. Everybody inside tumbled on top of one another until we were all piled up in the back of the ship.

Except for Nix. Somehow he stayed in place on the operating table. He was still asleep, snoring loudly.

Through the transparent wall, I watched the horizon bend. We were high enough that we could see the curve of the Earth.

"Uh, guys?" Dexter said as he floated away from us.

In fact, everybody was slowly floating toward the middle of the ship.

We were weightless.

Noah laughed as he spun in midair. Dexter and Totes kicked at each other, shooting themselves across the room.

Penny would've loved it.

Duncan wasn't too impressed, but why would he be? He's been a weightless ghost for over a year. "Been there, done that," he said.

For fifteen minutes, we played in zero g, almost forgetting the battle we were flying into.

Almost.

Before long, the ship began its descent on New York City. Gravity gently pulled our feet back down, and we all stood in front of the invisible wall, quietly watching the city grow larger. A line of tanks was crossing one of the bridges into the city, on its way to Times Square, no doubt.

"Great," Duncan said. "Now the army's involved."

Nobody said a word, but from the looks on everybody's faces, it was pretty obvious we were all feeling the same thing.

Fear.

CHAPTER TWENTY-NINE

"There's nobody down there," Dexter said as our ship hovered over Times Square.

He was right.

It looked like we were landing in a postapocalyptic movie, where all of humanity had died or disappeared.

The center of the square was empty, the cars in the streets abandoned. I'd never seen it like that, but to be fair, the only time I've ever seen it is when I stay up late to watch the ball drop on TV for New Year's.

And then I saw where all the people had gone. They were grouped on the side streets, walled off by police officers and their patrol cars.

I think all the smart people had hightailed it out of the city by now. The ones who stayed were the lookie-loos, hoping to catch some excitement. Every single one of them had their phones out, recording everything they could.

"Time to land this thing," Duncan said. "You think you can do it?"

"Yeah, there's literally a Land button," I said. "This ship is stupid-proof."

"Ben-proof," Dexter smirked.

Noah and Totes laughed.

That's fine. It's funny because it's true.

"Go ahead, then," Duncan said. "Right in the middle there."

"But that's in front of everybody," I said. "The whole *world* is watching!"

"We can't uncrack that egg. Donald knew this day was coming, Ben. It's sooner than he would've liked, but he knew it was coming." Duncan paused, putting a ghost hand on my shoulder and Noah's. It was faint, but I could actually *feel* his fingers. "And he would be *immensely* proud of you boys for being at the front of it."

I looked at Noah. Of the two of us, he's always been the levelheaded one. For the past two years, I'd been so distracted by my own stuff that I never even noticed what he had become . . . a *leader*.

Noah did the *"Aw, yeah"* nod, and then he said, "Let's land this bad boy."

I touched the Land button.

Our ship descended between the skyscrapers until finally settling on the ground. Through the transparent wall, I saw the Abandoned Children. William was standing close to the ship. Delilah, Vic, and Matthew were behind him, posted up around a red table and chairs. Penny sat in one of the chairs, scowling. She looked like she was more annoyed than afraid.

That's so Penny.

"Okay," I said. I was ready to try out this whole planning thing. "Two things could happen when we tell William that Donnie's gone. Either he's cool with it and sets Penny free, or he's *not* cool with it and we have to rescue her."

Noah shook his head. "A *million* things could happen, dude. What if he thinks we're bluffing? What if he never planned to let Penny go at all? What if this is all a trap? What if he's just gonna kill *all* of us?"

"Okay, yeah," I said. "I didn't think of *any* of that stuff."

"No matter what happens, our goal is Penny," Noah said. "Her safety is our endgame, even if it means putting *our* safety on the line."

Dang.

Noah was *born* to lead.

"Don't forget about Vic," Dexter said.

"Vic's a wild card," Noah said. "I don't know what she's gonna do."

"I'll get her back," Dexter said.

"But not until I say so," Noah said, pointing at Dexter.

"All right," he said.

"I don't think there's any way around it," Noah said. "William wants to put on a show for the world. It's why he picked *Times Square*."

"He *wants* a fight," I said.

"Yup," Noah said. "Things are going to get crazy no matter what, so let's be the ones who make it crazy—not them. That should catch him by surprise."

"How do we do that?" Dexter asked.

"William likes to talk," Noah continued. "So we'll let him talk, and when I give the signal, Dexter and I will start with the fire and ice explosions, as big as we can make them, all over the place. The second that happens, Ben and Totes will make a beeline for Penny."

Nix was still dozing on the operating table. I was gonna have to go out there without him—*not* good.

"Get Penny back to this ship," Noah said. "And then get back outside because William and his gang will still need to be stopped."

"And what's the plan for that?" Totes asked, concerned.

"Fight till one side loses," Noah said.

"Welp, it was nice knowin' y'all," Totes said.

"The goat's right," Duncan said. "Remember that William and Delilah aren't just powerful. They're *overpowered*."

"But if we leave, they'll tear up the city," Noah said. "So it's kind of our only option."

William and Delilah weren't like normal bosses in a video game. They were the nearly unbeatable ones in games that cheat. It was possible that we were walking out to our deaths, and the four of us knew it.

Noah held his fist out again. Totes, Dexter, and I bumped it one last time, and then we went out the door to meet William in the middle of Times Square.

CHAPTER THIRTY

We swaggered out of the ship like gladiators before a battle. Noah and Dexter walked on either
side of me while I rode on Totes. He normally hates giving rides, but he made an exception this time because
we had the most important job—rescuing Penny.

"My parents are gonna kill me when they see me on TV," Noah said.

"Darla's gonna *die* when she sees *me*," Dexter said.

"Ah, thank you guys for coming!" William said, looking genuinely delighted. "This place is so awesome, isn't it? I LOVE it here. Look, there's even a Disney store! I'm gonna get a BB-8 toy right after this."

He would've been a pretty cool guy if he didn't want to murder people.

"Welcome to the beginning of a new future!" he said, flexing his power.

All around us, tiny vortexes opened up, not big enough to do anything but pop some lightbulbs and slide some empty cars around.

"That's the clip they'll play over and over on TV," William said. He put his hands up like he was presenting a headline. "The Abandoned Children Take Control. Best. Rulers. Ever."

Dude was legit nuts.

"All right!" he said with a fist pump. "So where is the little guy?"

"First, I want to know that Penny's okay," I said.

William looked over his shoulder. "She's right there, unharmed, just like I promised."

"*Are you okay?*" I shouted to my friend.

Penny looked at me, like, "*Are you serious right now? I'm being held prisoner in the middle of Times*

Square!" Then she threw out the most sarcastic double thumbs-up I've ever seen.

"See?" William continued. "She's fine. So can we trade players now or what?"

"First, give us Penny," Noah demanded.

That was good.

If William handed Penny over first, then she wouldn't need saving. Hopefully it was gonna be as easy as that.

"Yeah, how about no?" William scoffed. "That's not how this works. First, *you* give us Donnie, *and then* we'll give you Penny."

Out of nowhere, Dexter offered a suggestion.

HOW 'BOUT WE TRADE 'EM AT THE SAME TIME?

Noah couldn't help but shoot Dexter a dirty look while I stared straight ahead, unflinching. Obviously we couldn't trade at the same time because we *didn't* have Donnie, but Dexter hadn't put those puzzle pieces together yet.

Dexter's eyes slowly grew larger as his brain caught up to what his mouth said. "Never mind," he mumbled.

"No, no, that's good," William said, beckoning his goons to bring Penny over. "We'll do it at the same time. Tell Donnie to come out of the ship, and let's get this over with."

Nobody said a thing.

Delilah, Vic, and the giant gecko led Penny over to us but stopped just behind their leader.

"Tell Donnie to come out and play!" William said, stomping his foot like a baby.

Dexter, Noah, and I looked back and forth at one another, hoping some sort of magical solution would present itself.

But it didn't.

We were stuck.

And it was obvious.

William huffed. "I mean, you *brought* him, right? He's on the ship right now, isn't he? You're just stalling because you hate the idea of anybody getting hurt? That *has* to be what you're doing, because it'd be *very* stupid if you were playing games with me."

I laughed nervously.

William sighed, eyes closed and head back. "I swear to God, I'll throw a car at you if you didn't bring him."

Might as well fess up. "So, about that . . ." I said. "We kind of don't have Donnie."

William became stone-faced, his stare piercing my soul. "What do you mean you *kind of* don't?"

"Right, not 'kind of,' but totally," I said. "We totally don't have him."

William grinded his teeth as the lizard-man put himself directly behind Penny. Delilah's fingertips buzzed with electricity. Vic took that as her cue to do something, too, so she floated a couple of inches off the ground.

"Donnie bailed on us!" I said.

"You're lying!" William shouted. "You're hiding him to protect him!"

"No, for real!" Dexter said. "We don't know where he is!"

William whipped his hands out like Dr. Strange, opening a vortex on the side of the street. The suction pulled a car off the ground and sent it sailing through the air straight for us.

"He was serious about the car," Dexter said.

It all happened so fast. There wasn't time to do anything except put our hands up—like that was gonna protect us from getting crushed by a four-thousand-pound car.

Then, out of nowhere, the car changed course, smashing into the ground right in front of us. We stumbled back as metal crunched and sparks flew from the asphalt.

It was hard to see what had happened through all the dust. Even William leaned in, trying to get a better look as the air cleared.

"Uh," Dexter said. "Is that what I think it is?"

Nobody answered.

Everybody was kind of in shock.

Well, everybody except for me.

Because it was the second time that day that I'd seen a giant shark out of water.

"Magnific!" I shouted.

"Ben Braver, *look* at you!" Magnific said, still in shark form. "All grown up and saving the day with your friends. I feel like a proud father! Well done, Beanie Weenie!"

"Why's everybody calling you that?" Noah said. "I feel like I'm missing something!"

"How'd you find me?" I asked Magnific. "But also— are you a *flying* shark?"

Magnific laughed as he morphed back into his human form. "I heard your name on TV and saw that Times Square was being attacked. So I called in a favor."

William stepped out from behind the crushed car. "Congrats, you almost got enough people for a fair fight."

Magnific puffed out his chest. "Turn yourself in now, Abandoned Child, and maybe we'll go easy on you."

"We?" William scoffed, rolling his eyes, but as his head craned upward, his face grew pale and his jaw dropped slightly.

Hovering above us were a dozen superheroes, all decked out in cool costumes and capes. The ones who couldn't fly were being lowered to the street by the ones who could.

If my life were a movie, this is where the music would've swelled with loud horns and huge drums. It was the epic-hero shot in real life.

"No way," Dexter said.

"Righteous," Totes whispered.

Noah just smiled.

Magnific winked at me. "Okay, so maybe I called in a *few* favors."

William and Delilah might've been overpowered, but now they were outnumbered.

We all waited for someone to make the first move. Supervillains on one side—superheroes on the other. It was the calm before the storm.

And then Matthew kicked things off.

He scooped Penny up with his tail, and that was it.

Time to rock and roll.

"Ben, go!" Noah shouted. "Now!"

"We'll hold them back for you, chum!" Magnific shouted as he charged forward, his friends following his lead.

Times Square erupted into an all-out battle of superpowers as explosions of fire burst overhead and hail rained down, shattering to pieces on the street.

Totes dashed across the battlefield so fast that I had to grab one of his horns to keep from falling off his back. Without Nix's powers, I was vulnerable to every single thing out there, and there was A LOT.

Fire. Ice. Vortexes. Lightning. A flying shark. Exploding asphalt chunks. Elastic arms. Water tornadoes. Blasts of energy. Warrior ghost ninjas raised from the dead. Mind-controlled insect armies. Lava monsters.

It was like a Power Battle cranked to eleven.

But most important, it kept William and Delilah busy.

Totes bum-rushed the lizard-man, smashing into his scaly rib cage. Matthew rolled over but kept his hold on Penny as she screamed, her power swelling and splashing drops of energy on the ground.

Matthew scurried to one of the buildings. If he went up the side, it would be impossible for us to follow.

"Oh no you don't!" Totes said, running faster than I'd ever seen him run. "Hang on, Braverboy!"

I wrapped my arms around the goat's furry neck as he rammed the lizard in the ribs again. That time I heard bones crack, but I couldn't tell if it was the lizard's ribs or Totes's horns.

Probably a little of both.

Matthew hissed in pain, dropping Penny. He spun around, furiously lashing out at us.

I slid off Totes's back as he stood up on his hind legs, waving his arms around and making noises like he was in a kung fu movie. *"Waaaa, psh! Psh, psh, psh! Ki-ya!"*

In his confusion, the gecko cocked his head, but that one second of distraction was all Totes needed. The goat spun around and donkey-kicked the lizard in the jaw so hard that *I* saw stars.

Matthew plopped down on the street, out cold. His body morphed back into a human.

"Totaaal knockout!" Totes cheered, hopping around his opponent with his front hooves in the air. *"I am the G.O.A.T! The Greatest Of All Tiiime!"*

The battle raged behind us as Penny jumped on Totes's back, her power dripping from her skin like sweat.

"Take her back to the ship!" I said, slapping Totes's butt.

"Dude," he said. "Inappropriate . . . but I'll allow it."

"Where are *you* gonna go?" Penny said.

"I'm going to help Noah and Dexter!" I said.

"Oh, cool, you got Nix on your head?"

"No."

"Then that's stupid!" she said. "Unless you *wanna* die?"

"I have to do something!" I said.

"Everybody out there has powers, and you don't!"

Penny said. "Totes is more qualified to fight than you are!"

Totes smiled proudly.

Ouch.

That one hurt.

It's all I ever wanted to be, but she was right.

This time, it was a dumb idea.

"Okay," was all I said.

I ran as fast as I could next to Totes, who was purposefully going slow enough that I could keep up. Penny was on his back, crouched low like a jockey in the Kentucky Derby.

Noah and Dexter were in the fight for their lives in the middle of Times Square. Magnific and his friends were powerful, but William was still able to hold *ALL* of them back with his vortexes. There must've been a dozen minivortexes he was controlling.

The real threat was Delilah. She was shooting out lightning bolts from *inside* a ball of electricity, which completely shielded her from harm. She had already taken out a couple of Magnific's friends.

Vic was still floating in the air. She wasn't fighting, but she wasn't running, either. I don't think she knew whose team she was on, which meant she hadn't fully given in to the dark side. Maybe there was still hope for her.

Dexter had transformed into a giant ice monster. In one hand, he had a shield that was actually the hood of a taxicab. With his other hand, he machine-gunned snowballs at Delilah's electric bubble.

Noah played it safe, circling high above the battlefield, dropping firebombs around William, but never straight up hitting him.

Totes, Penny, and I ran to the ship. I peeked in the door and saw Nix, still on the operating table, but at least he was sitting up.

Duncan swooped down from the sky. "Dexter and Noah need to fall back to the ship!" he shouted. "Those tanks are only a few blocks away! The army can handle it from here!"

I wanted to believe him, but I wasn't sure he believed himself.

That's when I heard a gut-wrenching scream through the chaos. No matter how much noise there was, I'd always recognize the sound of my best friend's painful cries. I turned around just in time to see Noah's body falling through the air, tiny bolts of electricity running over his skin.

He had been struck by one of Delilah's lightning bolts.

The other superheroes were too busy with the battle to notice that Noah had been hit. Nobody was gonna help him.

Without thinking, I ran toward my best friend, moving so fast that my shoes barely touched pavement. I couldn't fly up and catch him, but maybe I could break his fall if I got under him, the same way Duncan had saved my life once.

If this were a movie, time would slow to a crawl as Noah fell. The camera would look down on him so the audience could see the pavement grow closer. And then, at the last second, I'd appear in the frame to catch him and save his life.

But this wasn't a movie.

There was no slow-motion action sequence.

No epic music.

No cool camera angles.

There was only the obvious truth that I wasn't fast enough. Noah was gonna hit the ground, and there was nothing I could do.

The only reason we were out there was that I selfishly wanted to be the hero.

He was gonna *die* because of *me*.

And then, in that instant, I magically zoomed forward, skimming the ground faster than Noah was falling and crashing into my friend just before he landed.

We rolled across the asphalt as thick ropes wrapped around our bodies. When we finally stopped, we were on our backs, staring at the bright billboards hanging over us.

Noah coughed as he sat up. "What happened?"

I still wasn't sure myself, that is, until I heard Nix's voice in my head. *"S'up, buddy?"*

He was back.

And he was on my head right where he belonged.

"Dude, I am *so* glad to see you," I said. "Er, *hear* you."

"Let's save all that for later, huh?" Nix said. *"After we take care of these wads."*

I surveyed the scene.

Some of Magnific's friends had tapped out, taking refuge by Nix's ship because of how powerful Delilah and William were.

In a single bound, I landed next to Delilah.

She swung an electrified fist at me, but I used Nix's tentacles to flip around her before she could land the attack. She shotgunned another punch, but with Nix's power, it was easy to dodge.

I didn't need to fight back.

I only needed to keep her distracted.

And now that Delilah was all about me, Dexter closed in behind her. He gave it everything he had, pulling a plume of snow up from under her feet. With the snap of his fingers, the snow turned into solid ice, trapping her in a frozen prison, except for one tiny spot over her mouth where she could still yell a bunch of ugly stuff at us.

At that moment, Vic ran straight into Dexter's arms, and he hugged her just as tightly as he said he would.

With Delilah on ice, and Matthew TKO'd, William was the only one left.

"*That's enough!*" he said. With a thrust of his hand, a dark vortex opened over his head. He circled his arms, forcing the death tornado to rise higher and grow larger. Cars slid across the street, and even the buildings surrounding Times Square bowed at William's power.

"What're you doing?" I said.

"If you won't give me Donnie, then I'll *force* him to show up!" William said. "How much you wanna bet he'll magically appear if I destroy the world?"

My stomach sank as I suddenly understood. The Abandoned Children knew Donald Kepler changed history to save the world, and William was betting that Donnie would do the same thing.

But the only problem was that Headmaster Kepler came from the *future*, so he knew the world was gonna end. Donnie probably went *back* in time. He wouldn't have a clue about what William was doing.

The vortex was massive, looming, and silently terrifying—not loud with thunder and lightning, but peaceful like wind sifting through long grass.

I looked to Magnific and his buddies for help, but they were watching in shock, too hypnotized by the vortex of doom to do anything. Staring death in the face can make anyone's brain go blank.

"This isn't gonna work!" I said to William.

He put his fingers in his ears like a baby. *"I'M. NOT. LISTENING."*

I ran up and shoved him. "Donnie went *back in time,* so your plan isn't gonna work! It's just gonna destroy the world!"

William threw me to the ground. Then he clutched the hair on my head, except it wasn't my hair—it was the invisible Nix. The squid screamed inside my brain. William's grip on Nix was affecting my powers again.

"It'll work because he's a cheater," William seethed. "He'll show up to *chaaange* history. Just watch."

The city rumbled as some of the lighter abandoned cars began to rise off the ground. Billboards sparked as pieces ripped away, defying gravity and floating upward.

All I could do was watch the end of the world.

But then, all of a sudden, William let me go.

I fell on my knees as Nix's voice reappeared in my head. *"What's happening?"*

"I don't know," I wheezed.

When I looked up, I couldn't believe my eyes.

It was the last thing I expected to see.

It was Donnie.

"Ahaaaa!" William screamed as he ran toward him. "I *knew* you'd show up, you time-traveling cheater!"

But Donnie wasn't alone.

His parents were behind him.

And his mom had the Power Dampener.

Never mess with a mama bear's cub.

Mary squeezed the trigger of the crossbow, unleashing a glowing net that wrapped around William. He landed with a painful thud, unable to move or use his powers anymore.

With William's superpower in check, the vortex should've disappeared.

Except it didn't.

It was still swirling strong.

"Uh-oh!" William said with a laugh. "It's big enough to feed itself, and it's a hungry wittle baby!"

Donnie and his parents ran back to the ship with me. The other superheroes gathered around us.

"What in the blazes is that thing?" Richard asked.

"The end of the world if we don't stop it!" I said.

"How do we close it?" Dexter asked.

"By blowing it up," Duncan said. "Noah closed one back at the school with an explosion."

Noah pulled the same *Street Fighter* move he did back at the school, unleashing the biggest fireballs I've ever seen him make, but they were too small. Each one disappeared into the vortex like nothing.

Noah shook his head. "The explosion needs to be *bigger* than I can make." He turned toward Magnific and his friends. "Can any of you do that?"

"Not bigger than what you just tried, friend," Magnific said.

And then Noah looked at Penny.

Her eyes glazed over as she took a deep breath, and I knew exactly what she and Noah were thinking.

"No!" I shouted. "There's gotta be another way! Maybe this ship's got weapons!"

"*It doesn't,*" Nix said in my head.

The world was about to end, but that wasn't something I was worried about. That kind of thing was so huge that my brain figured it wasn't even possible, but Penny's death?

That was real.

Richard took a knee next to her. "Are you sure about this, darling? Nobody expects this of you."

She nodded bravely. "It's okay. I'm ready."

Was she saying she was ready to die?

I was pretty sure that's what she was saying!

"Penny, you can't!" I pleaded.

"Yes, I can," Penny said calmly, putting her hand on my arm. The glow in her skin had disappeared.

William was still in the street, watching the sky. "You're too late!" He laughed like a maniac.

Penny squeezed my arm. "But I need *you* to take me up there."

I didn't want that.

I don't think anybody wanted that.

But we didn't have a choice.

She was the only one who *MIGHT* be able to close the vortex. All she had to do was make herself explode the same way Angel did.

"Can you even do that?" I asked.

She shrugged. "Pretty sure it won't be hard," she said.

"What if your explosion is *too* big?" I said.

"Then the whole city goes up with it," Duncan said.

"But at least it'll only be the city and not the whole world."

He had a point.

A *terrible* point, but a point.

She put her arms around my neck as I hugged her tightly. Then I flew straight up toward the vortex in the sky.

The suction was stronger the closer we got. Instead of flying toward it, we were starting to get pulled into it.

Debris streamed past us, getting swallowed up by the eye of the vortex. I didn't know what was on the other side, but I sure didn't want to find out.

The glow from Penny's skin was still gone. She was doing a good job of keeping her power under control for the time being.

"*Fear versus love, fear versus love, fear versus love,*" Penny repeated to herself.

"What?" I asked, still making my way toward the eye of the monster.

"Mary and Richard said I have to let go of my fear, remember?" Penny asked. "I have to focus on love."

"It's a good thing I'm with you, then," I said, half-joking.

She stared into my eyes as a smile gently stretched over her face. Her skin instantly radiated stronger and cleaner than I'd ever seen before. There weren't any bubbles, no drops of energy leaking out.

She was an angel.

Her body grew hotter and hotter, but I couldn't stop hugging her. It was the last time I'd ever get to, and I didn't want to stop.

"Ben," she said. "You have to let go."

I loosened my grip, and she slid away slowly, but I held on until the last second, until it was only our fingertips that touched.

The suction of the vortex took her, and she drifted toward the center of it. Her entire body beamed with energy. She was the only light in all that darkness, but then she, too, disappeared, swallowed up in the eye of the vortex.

I stared, waiting for something to happen.

If Penny couldn't pull it off, the planet was done for.

Sure, that's bad, but the only thing I could think of was that Penny might possibly be dead at that moment.

And even though I'd be dead in just a few seconds, it pained me to know that I could've been with her for those few extra seconds.

But it never came to that.

The vortex lit up like the sun. The night sky turned bright yellow for a few seconds until it all faded back to black.

Penny had done it.

She had exploded.

Everything was back to normal.

The vortex had closed, and the planet was safe.

Times Square was in perfect shape.

I looked for Penny, hoping she had somehow survived the blast, but she was gone.

. . . *she was gone.*

CHAPTER THIRTY-ONE

Nope!

I was wrong.

Penny was still there; I was just looking in the wrong place! She was way under me, falling fast.

"*You should probably grab her!*" Nix shouted.

"On it!" I said, flying full speed.

I swooped down, carefully catching her. She was alive and smiling and everything. The glow in her skin faded as she hugged me.

I landed next to Nix's ship, but I didn't put her down. I would've held her forever if she let me.

Richard and Totes dragged William, Delilah, and Matthew aboard the spaceship.

Bystanders had pushed past the police barriers and were snapping millions of close-ups with their phones.

News crews swarmed the area, their cameras pointed at us as reporters tried to make sense of what just happened.

Magnific and his friends bid us a fond farewell and took off into the night sky.

My friends, everyone—Dexter and Vic *included*—stood with me in the middle of Times Square. We raised our hands to the crowd, and they just went nuts with cheers as our faces suddenly appeared on the screens above us.

We basked in glory, but not for long, because that's when the army showed up with their helicopters and tanks.

That was our cue to leave, pronto.

We ran back into Nix's ship, and I hit the Launch button for Colorado.

We were together.

We were safe.

We were heroes.

The world was never gonna be the same.

My face and my name were all over the news, along with the "Kepler Kids" and the "Abandoned Children."

Headmaster Archer made an official statement to try to keep ahead of the rumors. He spilled the beans on *almost* everything. The secret was out, and there was no sense in hiding it anymore.

So now the public knows people with powers live in their world, and if you ask me, they're pretty okay with it.

Some are scared, but most think it's just as awesome as I did when I first learned about it.

The only thing Archer kept secret was that Nix existed. Everyone who saw his ship on TV just thought it belonged to the academy, and Archer figured it was best to keep it that way. Superpowered people is enough to deal with. Throwing aliens into the mix would probably make heads explode.

"One thing at a time," he said.

William, Delilah, and Matthew were hauled off to the same place Abigail was taken to—the prison for the superpowered. I wondered what that even looked like.

Dexter and Vic were my friends now. *Good friends,* and they turned out to be two of the funniest people I've ever known.

Nix is leaving for home soon.

Am I bummed? Totally.

I would *love* it if he stayed and gave me superpowers whenever I wanted, but . . . he misses his family. His home. And he needs to get back to them. I knew that feeling better than anybody, so there was no way I'd stand in the way of that.

Besides, I'm over having superpowers. If there's one thing Magnific taught me, it was that I could do just as much, if not more, *without* powers. People need help, but you don't need superpowers to help them.

The Kepler family had the happiest ending of all of us. Richard and Mary aren't going back to 1963. They decided to stay in the present.

They didn't come to the decision randomly, though.

The history books say they disappeared in 1963, *after* their son vanished. Well, now we know where they went. They all traveled to the future—and *stayed* there. Richard and Mary will get to watch Donnie grow up now. They'll even teach at the academy while Donnie finally gets to attend it, fifty years after it opened. They get to be a family.

So we saved the world without anyone getting hurt.

Pretty awesome, if you ask me.

CHAPTER THIRTY-TWO

A week had passed since the Battle of Times Square, and everybody was behind the school to say good-bye to Nix.

We were all there—Donnie, Richard and Mary Kepler, Headmaster Archer, Professor Duncan, Totes, our parents, and even Dexter's sister, Darla, who had made the trip up to punch him in the arm for becoming cooler than her.

I explained everything to my parents, but they already knew most of it from TV. They were happy, but I could tell they just wanted me to come home to a normal life.

It was late, almost ten p.m., and we were gathered around a small bonfire. Penny strummed randomly on the uke her parents had brought from home at *her* request. She wasn't afraid of her power anymore.

The octo-bots that helped carry my luggage on the first day of sixth grade were inside Nix's ship with him, prepping it for takeoff.

I went into the ship.

Nix stopped what he was doing. "Thank you again," he said.

I acted cool. "Yup," I said. "Glad I could help. And now you get to go home."

"So do you," Nix said.

We sat in silence for a second.

Good-byes are hard.

Nix smiled. "I'm gonna miss you, Ben."

It seemed like he was stalling. Like he didn't want to go home just yet. But I wasn't gonna be the guy who asked him to stay. If he wanted to stay, then it had to be up to him.

I smiled back. "Me, too."

Is it weird to hug a squid?

Because that's exactly what I did.

A chorus of *awwwws* sang behind me. Everyone was in the doorway, watching this private moment.

"Shut up," I joked.

Just then, Penny's phone dinged from her pocket. She pulled it out and let out a gasp.

"What is it?" her dad asked.

"Another group of Abandoned Children just attacked Denver," she said, holding up her phone so we could see.

"There are superheroes to take care of that now," Duncan said.

"But it's only, like, ten minutes from here if we take Nix's ship!" Dexter said. "*We're* those superheroes!"

I looked back at Nix, but he wasn't there anymore.

Because he was already back on my head.

Nix paused and then got super serious. *"Ben . . . I will stay as long as you want me to."*

I looked at my parents for permission. My mom nodded at my dad as he sighed. "Fine," he said. "But be back before bedtime."

"Yessss!" I hissed.

"Am I just not here?" Duncan asked sarcastically. "Does anybody care that I disagree with this?"

Nobody answered.

"What're we waiting for?" Nix asked out loud. "People need our help!"

Penny gripped her uke by the neck and ran into the ship. Noah, Dexter, Vic, Totes, and Darla followed behind her.

"Yes, I'm going," Darla said to us. "And no, you can't stop me."

Nobody tried.

Richard joined us, too, but Donnie stayed with his mom. "Go get 'em," he said to us.

Noah took command. "Ben, you're on pilot duty. Get us to Denver."

I punched in the coordinates as Noah laid out the plan for what to do when we got there. After everybody outside was clear of the spaceship, I pushed my finger through the holographic Launch button.

My name is Ben Braver, and I am a *superhero*.

Nailed it.

ACKNOWLEDGMENTS

Thank you to all the awesome Ben Braver fans out there—you're the best!

Thank you to Connie Hsu for your support, expertise, and help with making sense of Ben's story. Time travel is hard! To Megan Abbate for your enthusiasm and your valuable insight—Ben and his friends wouldn't be as cool without you. To Elizabeth Clark for making this book come to life with your awesome design skills. To my publicist, Morgan Rath, for being so, so, so patient with me. To Tracy Koontz and Jill Freshney for you're rad copyediting skills.

To Dan Lazar for supporting all of my crazy ideas and for making all of this happen. To Torie Doherty-Munro, Cecelia de la Campa, and all the amazing people at Writers House who work so hard behind the scenes.

To Camye, Evie, Elijah, Parker, Finley, and Adler for being the reason I do this.

And last, but absolutely not least, thank you to ThunderCats, Silverhawks, Jayce and the Wheeled Warriors, Captain N: The Game Master, the Bionic Six, the Teenage Mutant Ninja Turtles, and that guy who turns into a car whenever it gets hot.

Marcus Emerson is the author of the hit Diary of a 6th Grade Ninja series, the Secret Agent 6th Grader series, and the Recess Warriors series. His career started in second grade when he discovered *Garfield*. He grew up playing *Super Mario Bros.*, watching *ThunderCats*, and reading comics like *X-Men*, *Superman*, and *Wildcats*. He lives in Eldridge, Iowa, with his wife and children.

marcusemerson.com